"I'm acting as your secretary."

"You're also female."

She arched mocking eyebrows, her lips tilting challengingly. "Am I?" she taunted. "I didn't think you had noticed!"

Raff simply looked at her. The intimate knowledge he had of her unclothed body was there in his gaze, and as he continued to look at her, Jane felt heat enter her cheeks.

Had she really thought, even briefly, that she could challenge this man? He would meet her challenge every time, and better it!

"What's the matter, Jane?" he said softly. "Are you starting to miss having a man in your life?"

CAROLE MORTIMER, one of our most popular—and prolific—English authors, began writing in the Harlequin Presents series in 1979. She writes strong traditional romances with a distinctly modern appeal, and her winning way with characters and romantic plot twists has earned her an enthusiastic audience worldwide. Carole Mortimer lives on the Isle of Man with her family and menagerie of pets. She claims this busy household has helped to inspire her writing.

Books by Carole Mortimer

HARLEQUIN PRESENTS PLUS

HARLEQUIN PRESENTS

Don't miss any of our special offers. Write to us at the following address for information on our newest releases.

Harlequin Reader Service
U.S.: 3010 Walden Ave., P.O. Box 1325, Buffalo, NY 14269
Canadian: P.O. Box 609, Fort Erie, Ont. L2A 5X3

CAROLE MORTIMER

Fated Attraction

Harlequin Books

TORONTO • NEW YORK • LONDON
AMSTERDAM • PARIS • SYDNEY • HAMBURG
STOCKHOLM • ATHENS • TOKYO • MILAN
MADRID • WARSAW • BUDAPEST • AUCKLAND

For
my husband, Frank

ISBN 0-373-11689-6

FATED ATTRACTION

Copyright © 1991 by Carole Mortimer.

Printed in U.S.A.

PROLOGUE

IN THE gutter.

Incredible. She, who until very recently, although she had taken it for granted at the time, had lived in the pampered, indulgent lap of luxury.

In the gutter.

Among the accumulated paper and empty cans, rainwater rushing by on its way to the drain several feet away, the rain continuing to fall heavily in the dimly lit street.

She couldn't even be bothered to get up. Her hip ached where she had landed on it heavily, and the throb in her ankle told her it was going to hurt too when she stood up and tried to put weight on it. So she wouldn't stand up, would just lie here and let the world, a world that had proved itself hard and unrelenting this last week, carry on without her. *It* didn't want her and, at the moment, *she* didn't want it!

How Jordan would laugh if he could see her now, unwanted, useless, completely defeated emotionally, and lying in the gutter while the rain fell and soaked her. It wasn't that he was a cruel man, it was just that his prediction that she would fail utterly on her own had proved correct. Even her suitcase had burst open when she had dropped it; all the beautiful clothes, that Jordan had told her time and time again that she spent too much money on, scattered over the road in the mud and the rain. So much for their 'designer labels' now!

She began to laugh, softly at first, and then more shrilly, laying back on the tarmac.

'That's all I need, a damned hysterical female!' rasped a voice that sounded more than a little impatient. 'Get up, woman, before another car comes along and finishes what I started!'

It was like having a bucket of ice-cold water thrown in her face, and she stopped laughing immediately, frowning up at the man who towered over her.

She had briefly forgotten, in her misery, the car that had turned the corner mere seconds ago, the suddenness of its appearance having been the reason she had stepped hurriedly back on the pavement, stumbling as she did so, the force of the water that sprayed over her as the wide tyres drove through puddles seeming to be the impetus needed to make her lose her balance completely, twisting her ankle as she landed heavily on her thigh.

The car had been brought to a halt some yards away, its back lights gleaming like red eyes in the darkness, the engine idly ticking over.

At least the driver had stopped.

Although there was no need for him to be so rude!

'If I could get up I would have done so,' she snapped. 'But you seem to have incapacitated me——'

'My car didn't touch you!' he bit out forcefully. 'You stepped off the pavement without looking, and when you realised there was a car coming you slipped trying to avoid it.'

It wasn't so far off the truth, but even so he didn't have to sound so arrogant about it.

'Your car hit her, anyone could see that,' a voice accused.

Amazing. Seconds ago this quiet back-street of London had been empty; now a small crowd had gathered to witness what they obviously hoped was going to be a scene.

The driver of the car glared at the man who had just spoken. 'As you were nowhere near the scene when the accident happened, I don't think that anything you have to say on the matter is relevant.'

Heathcliff. That was who this man made her think of. Dark and saturnine, with over-long hair that seemed inclined to curl, although it was difficult to tell with the rain streaming down his face— a face that was all dark hollows and shadows, his eyes glinting with anger.

Was she delirious? What did it matter who he made her think of? He was arrogant and condescending, and she had had enough of both emotions to last her a lifetime.

She moved gingerly, pain shooting through her ankle, her hip aching abominably. 'I don't think I can get up.' She gasped with the shock of the intensity of the pain.

'She's broken something.' That same accusing male voice in the crowd spoke with gloom. 'I don't think you should get up, love,' the man advised her confidingly. 'Wait until the police get here is what I say, and let them——'

'Police!' the driver echoed with scorn. 'There is no need to involve the police in this.'

'Of course there is.' The other man sounded scandalised—probably at the thought of seeing his evening's entertainment being cut short! 'You knocked this young lady down...'

'I did not knock——'

'Yes, you did!'

'No, I——'

'Oh for goodness' sake!' the 'young lady' cut in crossly, struggling into a sitting position to glare up at both of them, as no one actually seemed inclined to assist her. 'As you so rightly pointed out,' she snapped at the driver, 'if I don't soon get up off this road I'm going to be run over by other traffic and killed!'

'Here,' he bit out impatiently, his arms curiously gentle as he swung her up against his chest. 'Sorry,' he muttered as the movement caused her obvious pain. 'I will be seeing to this young lady's welfare,' he informed the crowd with finality.

Much to their disappointment, the 'young lady' noted ruefully, before she was briskly carried away to be placed on the warm leather passenger seat of the old-design Jaguar.

'My clothes!' she protested before he could slam the door behind her.

Irritation furrowed his brow once again before he glanced back at the suitcase and the strewn clothing.

'Hell!' he muttered with suppressed violence, closing her car door with the same controlled emotion.

But he did go back and pick up the clothes and push them haphazardly inside the case.

She watched his impatient movements in the wing-mirror, sure that the more delicate items of clothing—her bras and briefs were made of the finest silks—would be beyond salvation after his rough handling of them.

But the crowd had dispersed now, much to her relief, even the dogged heckler having taken himself off now that there wasn't any further fun to be had, at anyone's expense.

But, as the boot of the car was wrenched open and her suitcase flung inside, she realised how very alone she was with this man—a man who hadn't shown even a glimmer of a gentler side to his nature. He radiated barely controlled anger as he got in beside her, and she realised she couldn't get out of the car and get away from him even if she wanted to because her hip hurt her so badly and her ankle refused for the moment to support her weight, slight as it was.

If the man turned out to be some sort of kidnapper she didn't even think a ransom would be paid for her if it were demanded; she very much doubted that Jordan would pay to have her returned to him.

She might have been in the gutter a few minutes ago, filled with frustration and despair, but now she had a feeling she could be in danger!

CHAPTER ONE

'JANE SMITH!'

She kept her head held high, although she could feel the delicate colour slowly staining her cheeks at his scepticism of the name she had given the nurse at the hospital when that lady had come to take her details before she was seen by the doctor. She had sensed the derision of the man at her side then, but he had at least waited until they were alone before expressing his scorn.

She wondered what his feelings would have been if she had calmly announced her full name.

Which she had no intention of doing.

It was quite a mouthful, for one thing. Another factor dictating his reaction would be whether or not he had heard of her family. If he hadn't it wouldn't mean a lot to him. She had also learnt during the last week that using her full name, in certain circumstances, got her absolutely nowhere.

She had to admit she had been more than a little relieved when he had driven her straight to the accident department of this well-known hospital, although she knew without seeing the doctor that she hadn't actually broken anything, that she was probably just badly bruised. Although that felt painful enough.

She was just relieved she had been wrong about the 'danger' she had sensed. The man obviously couldn't wait to get rid of the responsibility of her!

In the bright lights of the hospital waiting-room he looked even more like her image of Heathcliff than she had first thought. His hair was very dark, not quite ebony, but a rich teak-brown, inclined to curl over the collar of his shirt and ears now that it was dry, eyes the colour of grey slate made even more vivid by the dark bronze of his skin. It was a strong face, unrelenting, and the darkness hadn't deceived about the hollows and shadows, his face all angles and deep grooves; character-lines, Jordan would probably have called them.

He looked slightly older than Jordan's thirty years, possibly in his mid-thirties, and the well-worn comfort of the Jaguar he drove was also evident in the worn denims and small-checked jacket he wore. A man who seemed to care little for his appearance, and yet at the same time there was something magnetically attractive about him, his masculinity undoubted, his virility tangible.

Older than her set, out of her experience, at least fifteen years her senior, and yet she felt a certain curiosity to know more about him. Strange...

He had to be married, of course, or possibly divorced. If he hadn't been one, or both, at his age, that surely only left—— No, she didn't for one moment believe his inclinations lay in that direction. He might find her an irritant, but that didn't mean he found all women so.

What would his wife, or ex-wife, be like? she wondered. Probably tall and blonde and athletically minded, as she was sure *he* was; he certainly didn't keep as fit as he looked by the odd game of golf, as many men tried—and failed—to do. Or maybe his wife hadn't shared his interests at all, maybe that was the reason they were divorced.

Ridiculous.

She had the man married and divorced, and she didn't even know *his* name!

'A good English name,' she stoutly defended what was, after all, part of her name. She stuck out her hand. 'I don't believe we've been introduced.'

His mouth twisted at her sudden formality given the circumstances, and Jane was made to see herself through his mocking eyes. Small and pert, with a body that could easily be called boyish in the fitted denims and bulky sweater, except that the full swell of her breasts was clearly discernible beneath the woollen garment, and her hair was a long, Titian— as the Duke of York chose to call this particular shade of hair that was also the colour of his wife's!—riot of virtually uncontrollable curls that reached almost down to her waist, more tangled than usual this evening after the rough treatment it had taken from the wind and rain outside. Sparkling blue eyes the colour of sapphires dominated the beauty of her pointed face, a face bare of its usual make-up because she had felt too despondent earlier to take the usual trouble with her appearance, utterly defeated, on her way back to Jordan and his 'I told you so's.

And instead of that she was sitting in a hospital waiting-room with a man who looked as if he would like to take that 'Titian'-coloured hair, wind it around her neck, and strangle her with it!

'Raff Quinlan,' he announced drily. 'And I have never cared to look into its origins.'

And he wasn't about to start now, his tone implied.

Raff Quinlan. Even his name was different, interesting.

Her hand dropped back to her side as he made no effort to take it in his much larger one. 'Am I keeping you from something?' Her voice was tart at the obvious snub.

He returned her gaze coldly. 'Yes.'

He wasn't just blunt, he was downright rude!

She drew in an angry breath. 'I didn't choose to be run down by your car...'

'My dear Miss Smith,' he exploded, grey eyes blazing angrily. 'I did not run you down with my car. You——'

'The doctor will see you now,' a young nurse cut in firmly, giving Raff Quinlan a reproving look as she wheeled the chair he had insisted on for Jane when they first arrived through to the examination-room. 'Would you like to accompany your wife?' she offered as an afterthought.

Wife? Jane raised her eyes heavenwards; as if they looked like a married couple!

Raff Quinlan obviously thought it a ridiculous assumption to have made, too, and was on the point of giving a scathing reply.

Some devil, probably the same devil that made Jordan call her impossible, made her smile sweetly at Raff Quinlan. 'I would rather you did come with me, darling,' she told him lovingly, adopting a forlorn expression designed to make him look guilty as she suddenly looked very sorry for herself. 'I'm a little nervous,' she added in a little-girl voice.

He looked ready to tell her exactly what he thought of this supposed nervousness, but the young nurse looking at him expectantly prevented him from doing that. His mouth set tightly.

'Of course—darling,' this last was added tightly, his movements controlled as he joined them.

Jane smiled up at him smugly as they went down the corridor to the examination-room. His expression promised retribution.

It came quicker than they had both expected, and from an unexpected quarter!

'Would you like to let your husband help you to undress and get up on the couch, Mrs Smith, while I tell the doctor you're here?' the nurse suggested briskly, not giving either of them chance to answer her as she swished out of the room.

Jane had always wondered how silence could possibly be deafening, but the silence that descended over the room once the door had closed, leaving her alone with Raff Quinlan, was definitely of that kind!

She dared a glance at Raff under her lashes, not fooled for a moment by his innocently concerned expression, knowing that his anger towards her had faded to be replaced by mocking amusement.

'Well, Mrs Smith?' he finally drawled, his humour somehow making him appear younger. 'Would you like me to help you take your clothes——?'

'Out!' she ordered firmly.

'But——'

'Out!' she repeated with finality, her level gaze brooking no argument.

'If you're sure...?' He grinned at her discomfort, taking his time about leaving the room, pausing at the door. 'I'll come back after a suitable period,' he taunted. 'The nurse already has her doubts about my husbandly concern: if I just disappear she'll think I don't give a damn... What was that?' he prompted at her mumbled remark. 'Did you say something, darling? I couldn't quite hear you, my love.' He raised dark brows as her mutterings continued.

'*Everyone* in this department will hear me if you don't leave soon,' she warned audibly.

His husky laugh echoed down the corridor, and Jane knew her own teasing had been more than successfully turned back on her. Jordan wasn't capable of understanding her humour, let alone returning it; to be honest, this bantering made a pleasant change. Not that she was about to let Raff Quinlan know that—he was altogether too arrogant already.

Actually, she almost instantly regretted his having left the room, quickly discovering that the bruising to her body was so bad now every movement was an agony. Any help easing off the bulky sweater and denims would have been welcome, even Raff Quinlan's, by the time she had struggled out of her clothes and slipped beneath the sheet on top of the examination-couch, tears wetting her cheeks in painful silence.

On top of everything else, she felt sick.

Raff took one look at her when he came into the room, and picked up the kidney-shaped dish that stood on the side-table, reaching her side just in time for her to empty the contents of her stomach into it.

She fell back against the pillow once the retching had stopped. 'I'm sorry,' she groaned self-consciously.

'Don't be,' he dismissed easily, crossing the room as she closed her eyes weakly.

Jane didn't blame him for walking out in disgust; she couldn't bear to see anyone being sick, herself. She must have been more shaken by the fall than she had realised.

Her eyes opened in surprise as she felt a damp cloth against her forehead and down over the heat of her cheeks. Blue eyes looked straight into grey, so close she could see the long length of Raff Quinlan's lashes.

'I thought you had gone,' she told him huskily.

'No, I—God, you look awful!' He shook his head, frowning darkly.

She closed her eyes again, smiling faintly. 'Thanks!' she grimaced.

'I just hadn't realised——'

'Mrs Smith?' A young man with hair almost as red as Jane's came into the room, followed by the nurse. 'I'm Dr Young,' he introduced himself confidently.

Jane had already guessed that; possibly because of the badge attached to the white coat he wore that bore the name 'Dr P Young' upon it!

'I'm not *Mrs* Smith!' She was tired of that game now.

'Ah,' the doctor nodded. 'Then the two of you aren't married?'

Obviously! She was being impossible, and she knew it. If only she didn't feel so sick.

'No,' she sighed.

'Well, it doesn't matter,' the doctor dismissed briskly. 'The point is, you want Mr...? He looked enquiringly at Raff.

'Quinlan,' he instantly supplied.

'Right,' the younger man said before turning back to smile reassuringly at Jane. 'All that matters is that you want Mr Quinlan in with you during the examination.'

'But I——'

'I'm going to be here,' Raff cut in firmly, his steady gaze meeting hers with determination.

To be quite truthful, the nausea, and its subsequent result, had tired her to the point where she really didn't care any more. She very much doubted she would be the first—or the last!—woman Raff would see in her bra and briefs. She tried to remember the colour of the underwear she was wearing today, but for the moment it eluded her; she did know it would match in colour, whatever that colour was. It was one of her foibles... And extravagances, Jordan would have said. Oh, damn Jordan and his preaching! It was doing little to ease the pain as the doctor examined her ankle!

'Hm.' He frowned a little. 'Just badly bruised, I think. Although we'll X-ray it anyway,' he announced cheerfully. 'Just to be on the safe side. Your hip was the other place injured, I believe?' He briskly pulled the sheet down to examine the injured area.

Jane heard Raff's sharply indrawn breath, wondering if she could have been wrong about his having seen a woman in her underclothes before.

She looked across at him curiously, but his gaze was fixed on the area being examined by the doctor. A glance down at that spot herself told her why!

She knew her hip was extremely painful; in fact the nausea had begun in the car on the drive here from the pain of it. But she had just been concentrating on getting her outer clothing off earlier without fainting, and hadn't had the strength to actually look at her hip. She wished she hadn't bothered now either!

Her side was black and blue with bruising already, not just on the hip-bone but across her stomach and down her thigh too. It looked ghastly. No wonder Raff was staring.

Just when she thought she couldn't stand the poking and prodding into her flesh any longer the doctor straightened.

'Well, it looks as if you've been quite lucky, young lady.' His smile had gone now to be replaced by a reproving frown. 'I don't think any bones have been broken here either. You sustained the injuries in a fall, I think you said?'

'Yes,' she nodded distractedly. 'I tripped and fell over the pavement.'

The doctor continued to frown. 'The injuries seem rather—severe, for a fall of that nature.'

'Well, I——' Colour flooded her cheeks as she sensed concern behind the question. She glanced at Raff, his mouth tight now as he too sensed the scepticism. My God, the doctor didn't really think that . . .! She respected his concern, realised that he probably often had reason for it, but it really was unfair to Raff in the circumstances.

'I fell in the street and Mr Quinlan very kindly helped me by driving me here,' she told the doctor firmly. The last thing she wanted was to get involved with the police over what had, after all, just been an accident.

The doctor still didn't look convinced, but there was really very little he could do about the situation in the face of her insistence. 'We'll X-ray the ankle and hip just to be sure,' he told her gently. 'And decide what to do with you once we have the result of those.'

That sounded rather ominous. What did he mean, 'decide what to do with her'?

She wasn't given the chance to ask either the nurse or the doctor that question before they bustled out of the room in deep conversation together, the doctor presumably on his way to treat another patient, the nurse to organise Jane's X-rays.

Jane couldn't quite look at Raff after the implication the doctor had made about him a few minutes ago.

He crossed the room to stand next to her. 'I had no idea you were so badly marked,' he spoke quietly.

She grimaced dismissively. 'I bruise easily.'

He shook his head. 'You must have fallen very heavily. Or else I did actually hit you with the car...'

'No,' she denied as she sensed the doubt in his voice. 'I only said that earlier because I was annoyed by your bluntness,' she explained truthfully.

'Nevertheless, if I hadn't driven around that corner at speed——'

'You weren't speeding,' she cut in exasperatedly.

'But——'

'Mr Quinlan,' Jane spoke steadily. 'Believe me, my accident was not your fault.'

His mouth was tight. 'Nevertheless, I'm responsible for you...'

'I'm responsible for myself!' Her tone was a little more vehement than the occasion warranted, but she was more than a little tired of being told she wasn't capable of taking care of herself. She certainly wasn't anyone's *responsibility*. God, what an awful label to give someone! 'I'm grateful to you for bringing me here.' She spoke more calmly now. 'But there's really no need for you to delay yourself any longer.'

'I was only on my way back to my home,' he said dismissively, his gaze once again on the brightness of her hair.

'Then your wife——'

'I'm not married,' he bit out curtly.

Jane couldn't help but wonder why that was. Unless, as she had presumed earlier, he had been married and divorced. It was the most likely explanation. For a man who supposedly lived alone he had been in a hurry to get there earlier.

Something about this man raised her curiosity, possibly because she sensed there was no artifice in him—not even the one of politeness! Jordan would find him brash in the extreme, but then Jordan could be brash himself on occasion.

'Nevertheless,' she said firmly, 'the X-rays will take some time, and I really mustn't keep you any longer.'

'You——'

'Don't bother to dress, Miss Smith.' The nurse came back into the room, straightening up Jane's discarded clothes. 'We need you undressed for the X-ray, anyway.'

Jane had had no intention of even attempting to put her clothes back on in front of Raff Quinlan, even if she hadn't been hurting so badly that the nausea was never far away.

Perhaps the hospital just wasn't busy, or maybe it was the time of night, but the X-rays were completed and a diagnosis given within a matter of minutes; there were no bones broken, only the severe bruising. But even that was enough to make Jane shudder at the thought of putting her clothes on again.

Some of her distress must have shown on the paleness of her face.

'Of course, I think we should offer you a bed for the night,' the young doctor smiled encouragingly. 'If only as a precaution.'

For 'offer her a bed' Jane knew he meant admit her to the hospital, and she had no desire to spend the night in a hospital ward. But she was sure the doctor was as aware as she was that the address she had given them was that of a hotel, a hotel she had actually booked out of earlier today.

'Is that really necessary?' Far from leaving, Raff had gone with her to the X-ray department, and then stayed right by her side while the doctor gave her his verdict on her injuries. Now he spoke with a quiet authority. 'As long as Miss Smith has someone to take care of her, couldn't she be allowed to leave?'

The doctor looked slightly irritated by this interruption, obviously still not quite convinced of the other man's innocence in the affair, although he was holding a tight check on any more even veiled accusations of that nature. 'I suppose so,' he accepted slowly. 'But as she——'

'Miss Smith has somewhere to go,' Raff told him arrogantly.

Even Jane looked at him in some surprise. If that 'somewhere' was his home, then he could forget it; she may be weak but she wasn't helpless.

But if seeming to agree to that suggestion would get her out of here without too much fuss she could always make other arrangements once they were outside. After all, she didn't have to go anywhere, do anything she didn't want to do. After years of being ordered around she was finally free to make her own choices. Even if the majority of them this last week had been a disaster!

'Miss Smith? Miss Smith?' The doctor repeated his query more firmly at her wandering attention.

She looked up to find them all looking at her—the nurse kindly, the doctor enquiringly, Raff Quinlan challengingly. It was the latter that now held her attention.

'Is Mr Quinlan's suggestion agreeable to you?' the doctor persisted.

The poor man was still half convinced she had taken a beating from Raff Quinlan!

And Raff was still fully aware of the unspoken accusation.

'Yes, it's agreeable to me,' Jane finally answered, much to Raff's unspoken but felt relief, and the doctor's chagrin.

But he seemed to be resigned to her decision as he stood up to leave. 'If you have any further trouble, don't hesitate to either come back here or see your own doctor,' he advised.

'By "further trouble", I suppose he meant any more beatings from me,' Raff muttered grimly in the darkness, Jane now seated next to him in the

Jaguar, their departure from the hospital made without further incident after the nurse had carefully helped her to dress.

In truth Jane felt slightly lethargic now, the doctor having prescribed pain-killers to at least help ease some of her discomfort. The last thing she felt like doing now was sorting out a hotel for the night. But it had to be done. Raff Quinlan's ruffled feelings over the doctor's implications was the least of her worries for the moment.

She looked about her in the darkness, realising they were fast leaving town—Raff's home, wherever it was, seeming to be far from the hotels of London.

'If you pull over at the next corner, I can get a taxi back to a hotel,' she told him sleepily, those tablets, whatever they were, making her feel very tired.

He didn't even glance at her. 'I said you had somewhere to go,' he said tersely. 'And you do. You also have someone to "take care of you".'

'You?' Jane scorned, her lids becoming so heavy now she could barely keep them open.

'If necessary,' he nodded abruptly.

'It isn't,' she said drily.

He gave her a scathing glance. 'Forgive me if I disagree with you.'

Her mouth tightened at the insult. 'No.'

'My dear young lady...'

'I'm not your *dear* anything,' Jane snapped. 'And I have no wish to go to your home.'

His mouth twisted. 'You talk as if you usually expect your wishes to be carried out without question.'

Perhaps she did, but she had a feeling, from the little she had learnt of this man this evening, that he rarely considered anyone else's wishes but his own!

'I want you to stop the car immediately so that I don't have too far to walk before I can get a taxi back into town,' she told him firmly, although she was aware that her voice sounded less than convincing, and that she was feeling sleepier and sleepier by the moment.

Raff Quinlan laughed softly. 'You don't look capable of standing on your feet, let alone walking anywhere.'

'I am—capable, of doing—whatever I have to—do...'

It was the last thing she remembered saying, sleep finally overcoming her as she slumped down in the car seat.

CHAPTER TWO

WHAT on earth . . . ?

Where was she? Jane felt panicked as she awoke fully and didn't recognise her surroundings. She had been on her way to a hotel—but this wasn't a hotel, she felt sure of it.

God! The pain when she tried to move . . .

And with the pain came the return of her memory. The headlights of the car. The pain in her ankle as she turned to hurry back on to the pavement, then the terrible jarring of her hip as she made contact with the hard road.

Raff Quinlan . . .

She remembered everything about him too now— the way he towered over her in the darkness, his arrogance, his rudeness, the way he had insisted on bringing her to his home despite her protests . . .

She was almost afraid to look beneath the bed-clothes, had a feeling she already knew what she was going to find. Nevertheless she closed her eyes, took a deep breath, and lifted the sheet.

Naked.

Completely.

Even the peach-coloured underwear was missing now.

There was something vaguely disturbing about the thought of someone undressing her when she was unconscious from the effect of pain-killers and tiredness because of shock—unfair somehow, and it gave Raff Quinlan an advantage over her that she didn't like. At the hospital she had been wearing no less than if she had been on a beach, but being stripped naked when she could do nothing to prevent it was—well, it was underhand.

And Raff Quinlan was responsible, somehow she felt sure of that. After all, he had admitted he didn't have a wife who could have done it.

She looked up sharply as the bedroom door opened after a brief knock.

'Ah, good morning, my dear!' A tall woman in a tailored blue dress with a pristine white collar bustled into the room carrying a silver tray that held what looked like a pot of coffee. 'I hope I didn't wake you.' She smiled brightly before putting the tray down on the bedside-table and straightening, a perplexed frown appearing between her eyes as she looked down at Jane.

'I didn't realise—— For a moment you looked so much like——' She broke off, shaking her head. 'I'm sorry, for a moment you looked so much like—someone I used to know.'

Her smile was only a little strained now. 'I haven't even introduced myself,' she scolded self-derisively. 'I'm Mrs Howard, Mr Quinlan's housekeeper.'

And she had obviously never seen Jane before this moment, confirming that she hadn't been the one to undress her the evening before!

But, remembering the evening before, Jane realised she had started a deception with Raff Quinlan that she would now have to carry on. 'Jane Smith,' she supplied gruffly.

'Cream and sugar?'

'Sorry?' She looked up with a frown, the frown clearing as she realised the housekeeper was pouring her a cup of coffee. 'Oh. Both. Thank you,' she accepted with a tight smile.

What was that saying, 'When first you practise to deceive'...?

Sitting up to actually take the offered cup of coffee wasn't as easy as it should have been, either. Every movement caused her pain, and there was her nakedness to consider. Not that she was at all shy about that, she just didn't know what explanation Raff had given this woman for her being here, and her nakedness might look a bit suspect, in the circumstances. If Raff had felt he owed his housekeeper an explanation at all! Somehow she doubted it.

'Jane Smith?'

Her frown returned as she looked up from securing the sheet more firmly about her breasts, not quite as awake as she would have liked to have been, the pain-killers seeming to have left her with a slightly muzzy feeling in her head.

She took the coffee-cup from the other woman, spilling some of the hot liquid into the saucer as her hand shook slightly. 'Sorry,' she grimaced. 'This is much appreciated.' And it was, for her mouth felt like sandpaper.

She decided to ignore the reference to her name; it had already been discussed enough, one way or another! But sipping the coffee made her realise she had a sudden *urgency* to find a bathroom!

Her suitcase was just visible behind the bedroom chair, and she had no reason to suppose any of her things had been unpacked and placed in the spacious drawers of the dresser. And, unfortunately, the last time she had seen the wrap she had brought with her it had been strewn across the road soaking up muddy water like a sponge. In fact, most of her clothes had been doing the same thing. But she could hardly stay in this bed forever!

In fact, she couldn't stay in it another minute longer, with her predicament becoming more and more desperate by the second!

'My dear?' Mrs Howard seemed to sense her discomfort, if not the reason for it.

Jane's smile was strained. 'I don't seem to be wearing a nightgown, and—well, I need to...'

'Oh, my dear, how thoughtless of me!' The other woman instantly looked contrite. 'Your things are all laundered downstairs. Mr Quinlan explained about the catch breaking on your case, and all your beautiful clothes getting muddy. I'll just pop down and get them,' she reassured her.

Jane waited only as long as it took the other woman to leave the room before struggling out of bed and into what she could see was the adjoining bathroom.

She was more than a little shaky on her legs, and each movement across the room was an agony, but she finally made it, her relief immense once she had done so.

She could think clearer now too and, although her accident the night before had delayed her returning home to Jordan, it had only done so for that one night; now she would have no choice but to go back. She had been so sure she could succeed on her own a week ago, but now she was defeated, knew he was right—that she needed him and the money to survive.

She closed her eyes in shame at the pained memories of the last week—of one rejection after another, one humiliation after another. She had been so sure she could look after and support herself, and instead she had found how ill-fitted she was to do the latter, at least. And without the qualifications and means to support herself she wasn't capable of being independent.

Of course, there were a lot of young women in London who couldn't get a legitimate job and who therefore found some other means of supporting themselves, but even going back to Jordan had to

be better than that alternative. Better the devil she
knew than ones she didn't know, she had decided
last night when she'd packed up to go home. Much
as she hated the thought of Jordan's gloating self-
satisfaction in being proved right about her depen-
dence upon him.

The housekeeper still hadn't returned to the
bedroom by the time she had finished in the
bathroom, and so Jane hobbled as best she could
across the room, giving a gasp of horror as she
caught sight of her reflection in the dressing-table
mirror. Her hip seemed to have turned all the
colours of the rainbow now, the bruising having
spread further and deepened.

She might not want to stay in bed, but she wasn't
sure she was going to be able to bear the pressure
of normal clothing against her tender flesh.

She looked at her reflection critically, trying to
see her body from a man's point of view. Her skin
was quite tanned—it was summer, after all—and
she had the usual smattering of freckles that most
people with her colouring were afflicted with, although not so many that it could be thought un-
attractive. Firm breasts were tipped with delicate
coral pink, fuller than her other slenderness would
imply, but proudly uptilting. Her waist was slender,
her hips boyish, her legs surprisingly long and well-
shaped for her five-feet-two-inch height. Like a
long, leggy filly, Jordan always said.

Jordan. Jordan. Jordan. She had never realised before quite how much notice she took of the things he said to her.

'You really are a bloody mess, aren't you?' said an impatient voice from behind her.

A voice she recognised only too well!

She gave a yelp of dismay before crossing the room to the sanctuary of the bed and the protective bedclothes, and looking accusingly at Raff over the top of the snowy-white sheet.

She hadn't heard his approach or the bedroom door opening, but there he stood, larger than life in the daylight, the fitted denims low down on his hips, the dark blue shirt he wore making his eyes look darker.

But he still made her think of Heathcliff, his dark hair tousled and inclined to curl, his skin ruggedly tanned.

'Here.' He held up the clothes that were draped over his arm, derisively taking pity on her. 'But I've seen it all before, you know,' he drawled mockingly.

In Technicolor!

Her cheeks felt hot at the thought of this man's hands on her body. Had her nakedness left him unaffected? Probably. He didn't give the impression he found her in the least attractive. It wasn't the reaction men usually had to her vivid colouring.

'In that case——' she sat up on the bed, baring her shoulders and back '—pass me my robe, would you?' She held out her hand for the garment, her gaze unflinching.

Admiration slowly darkened his eyes and, although slow in coming, he actually smiled! 'I wonder just who you are, Jane Smith?' he mused softly.

Her head went back at this direct challenge, her defensive action turning to puzzlement as his expression became harsh, and his narrowed gaze rested on the flowing fire of her hair as it fell forward across her breasts.

'I mean to find out before you leave here,' he told her curtly.

Jane felt a shiver of apprehension, instantly dismissing the emotion as being ridiculous. She didn't know exactly where she was, but she could leave any time she wanted to. Couldn't she...?

'Where did you come from last night?' Raff demanded to know. 'Where were you going *to*?'

'I don't think that's any of your business,' she snapped resentfully, well aware of what a disadvantage she was at, her robe having been placed over the back of the bedroom chair with her other clothes, way across the other side of the room. As Raff very well knew!

His eyes were still narrowed, his arms crossed in front of the broadness of his chest. 'You gave your address at the hospital last night as being a hotel, but you must have lived somewhere before staying there?'

He was being deliberately provocative, almost insulting. 'Raff...'

'Who was he, Jane Smith?' he pushed, not waiting for her to finish.

'Who was who?' Jane frowned.

'Your wealthy lover!'

'My——?' Jane choked with indignation. 'What on earth are you talking about?' she gasped.

He shrugged. 'I may not know too much about ladies' clothing——' his mouth twisted derisively '—but even I recognise some of the labels in your clothes as being designer models. Who bought them for you?'

'I don't have to——'

'It was a man, wasn't it?' he cut in forcefully. 'Silken underwear——' He held up one of the lacy bras Jane favoured, that minute scrap of expensive lace looking even smaller in his callused hand. 'Bought to please a lover. Or by him,' Raff added hardly.

In truth, each and every article of her clothing had been paid for by a man, but she had chosen the underwear to please herself, no one else, loving the silken feel of it against her skin.

She shook her head. 'You don't know what you're talking about.'

'Don't I?' he rasped, throwing the bra down disgustedly on top of her other clean clothing. 'Believe me, I know more than you think,' he told her heavily. 'But before this goes any further I think I should tell you I'm not on the lookout for an expensive mistress. Or one of any other kind, come to that,' he added insultingly.

His behaviour took her breath away, angry colour darkening her cheeks. 'If I *were* on the lookout for a rich lover, you can be sure you wouldn't even be a consideration!'

Really, the man didn't even know her, and yet he could make accusations like that!

'Then we understand each other,' he nodded with satisfaction.

'Completely,' she snapped resentfully.

'Good,' he said smugly. 'Now that we're agreed on what neither of us want, we can get around to discussing what I *do* want.'

'Sorry?' Jane shook her head, still feeling slightly muzzy. It must be those tablets she had taken the night before. Maybe she was imagining this whole conversation? It was too outrageous to be real!

'Can you type?' He sat down in the bedroom chair, uncaring that he crushed her clothes in doing so.

Jane frowned, having difficulty keeping up with the conversation now. 'Type?' she repeated dazedly.

'Yes.' His mouth twisted. 'You know, place your fingers on the keys of a typewriter and make words appear on——'

'I'm well aware of what typing is,' she snapped. 'I just don't see what it has to do with me?'

Raff looked at her consideringly. 'At a guess, I would say right now you're homeless and job-less——'

'That's a hell of an assumption to make,' Jane bit out resentfully. God, was she so transparent? Possibly, to this man, with his probing eyes and cynicism. Although he certainly wasn't a hundred per cent right about her! Just enough to have un-nerved her, she admitted.

She still had no idea where she was, and al-though Mrs Howard had seemed respectable enough that was really little comfort right now.

Raff arched dark brows. 'But a correct one?'

'Who are *you*, Raff Quinlan?' Her head was back challengingly.

He shrugged broad shoulders. 'Rafferty Quinlan. Thirty-seven. Divorced.' The last was added bit-terly. 'In charge of the running of an estate that is slowly bleeding itself—and me—dry!'

It was the very briefest of résumés, and yet Jane was able to glean a lot from it. His marriage, whether it had initially been a happy one or not, had ended badly, which might account for some of his behaviour towards her. But not all of it!

' "In charge of running an estate"?' she repeated slowly.

He nodded abruptly. 'I can't exactly claim to own it when it's mortgaged up to the hilt,' he rasped. 'My father had little interest in the place for years before he and my mother were killed in a plane

crash five years ago, and he had let things deterio-
rate badly. My darling wife decided she didn't want
to be stuck out in the middle of Hampshire struggling to make a living, let alone enjoying herself,
and took what little there was left as a divorce
settlement. I've only managed to keep Mrs Howard
because she's run the house since before I was born,
and considers it more her home than I do!'

Jane didn't believe that; she sensed a fierce pride
in Raff in the estate he called his home.

And at least she knew where she was now! Not
that she was too familiar with Hampshire, but she
felt a little more reassured now that she was at least
approximately aware of her whereabouts.

Raff's wife couldn't have loved him if she could
have walked out on him for such a reason. And it
would probably explain part of his resentment towards the type of woman he had decided she had
to be.

But it didn't explain his conversation of a few
minutes ago.

'What does all this have to do with whether or
not I can type?' She frowned.

His mouth twisted. 'Well, as it seems for the
moment I'm responsible for you...'

'You most certainly are not!' she protested indignantly. 'I'm responsible for myself,' she told him
firmly.

At least, she was trying to be.

Her bank account stood at nil and, for all that she tried to deny it to this man, she was homeless into the bargain; she hadn't even thought to bring any of her jewellery—that she could have sold and lived off the money for a while—away with her when she'd left.

'You aren't doing a very good job of it,' Raff drily echoed at least some of her sentiments.

'I'm doing the best that I can!' To her chagrin she heard her voice break with emotion.

Raff looked at her closely, obviously having heard that emotion too. 'We all do that, little one,' he told her softly. 'It just isn't always enough.'

No, she acknowledged sadly, it wasn't always enough...

She didn't even want to think about Jordan sitting waiting for her to crawl back and tell him he had been right about her not being able to survive on her own.

She blinked back the tears. 'I'll make your problems one less by leaving here as soon as I've ordered a taxi.' She didn't think Jordan would mind paying the fare; it would be worth it to him to have been proved correct!

'To go where?' Raff's eyes were narrowed. 'Back to him?'

Her cheeks were flushed. 'I told you——'

'Surely working for me, once you've ceased being a walking bruise, of course—even I'm not that much of a taskmaster that I would expect you to

work while you're still in pain . . .!' he derided what
he had guessed had been her opinion of him '. . . has
to be better than returning to a man you obviously
have no desire to go back to!' he said exasperatedly.

'What do you know about how I—work?' Jane
repeated slowly as all of his words sank in. 'What
sort of work are you talking about?' she asked
suspiciously.

His mouth twitched. 'Well, I've asked you if you
can type—so I obviously want you to start cooking
for me!' He shook his head. 'What sort of work
do you think I mean?' he scorned.

Work. Raff was actually offering her a job! But
why? He had treated her as nothing but a nuisance
since he had first met her. Probably because she
had been one, she ruefully acknowledged. He
wasn't the type of man to take lightly having his
life interrupted as disastrously as last night had
done. But he also wasn't a man to shirk what he
considered his responsibility either.

Responsibility. How she was coming to hate the
very sound of that word!

She looked up at Raff uncertainly. 'By working
for you, do you mean——?'

'I can afford to pay you a small wage, plus your
room and food, if that's what you're worried
about,' he cut in harshly, his eyes narrowing resentfully. 'The estate may be in difficulties, but I'm
not bankrupt yet.'

And she had obviously hit upon a very raw nerve!

But the offer of a job was so tempting. Any job. It was exactly what she had been looking for, praying for. It meant so much more to her than just no longer being dependent upon Jordan. Not that she intended telling Raff Quinlan about *that*.

She looked at him quizzically. 'Why?'

He gave an impatient sigh, as if already regretting having made the offer at all. 'Don't think I would be doing you any favours, Jane Smith,' he rasped. 'I have correspondence that needs answering dating back three months or so, have been so tied up with work on the estate these last few months that I just haven't had time to tackle answering any of the mail.'

She frowned. 'You usually do the typing yourself?'

Not that he didn't look capable of coping with any problem that came his way—it was just unusual for a man in his position; she certainly couldn't see Jordan doing his own typing, no matter what the circumstances!

Raff gave a dismissive shrug. 'I have an aunt who comes down from town occasionally and does it, mainly so that she can keep an eye on exactly what's going on here,' he added derisively. 'But she hasn't found the time recently in her busy schedule.' The last was said sarcastically.

Jane wasn't the world's best typist, as the last week of job-hunting has proved, although that was mainly because it was a lot of years since she had attempted any typing at all; but if Raff didn't mind her lack of speed she was at least accurate.

My God, she wasn't seriously thinking of accepting his offer, was she?

What did she know about the man—other than the fact that he seemed to be a law unto himself? She didn't even know exactly where she was, let alone anything else.

And yet...

A job was all she needed. Just for three months. Until August the thirty-first. And there was Mrs Howard; she had seemed respectable enough...

Raff stood up abruptly. 'Think about it,' he bit out tersely.

'Oh, but——'

'I've wasted enough time already for one morning,' he continued harshly. 'Maybe when you decide what you're going to do you'll let me know?' He strode across to the door, emanating physical power, stopping to turn back to her. 'But I would advise you to consider very carefully before returning to a situation that was obviously stressful enough for you to have left it in the first place.'

And with that last, strangely gentle advice Raff left the bedroom.

Jane dropped back on to the pillows, totally dazed by this complex man. One minute so harsh and dismissive, the next almost caring. But of course he didn't care for her, just felt a *responsibility* towards her because of last night.

But did that really matter?

If she accepted his offer of a job she wouldn't be cheating him in any way, would work as hard as she was capable of, and they would both be getting something out of the situation—Raff a backlog of correspondence that was troubling him, and she—well, ultimately she would get so much more out of it.

But was this a frying-pan-into-the-fire situation? Wasn't Raff more of an enigma to deal with even than Jordan?

But it was only for three *months*, she reminded herself again. What other offers had she had?

None.

Her whole situation could be completely turned around if she just agreed to work for Raff Quinlan...

Was that too high a price to pay for proving Jordan wrong?

She had left him so confidently, so sure she could support herself. And she could—if she just took the job Raff offered her...

Pride warred with necessity—and finally necessity won. She couldn't let it bother her that Raff had only offered her the job because he felt he had rescued her like some stray from the street. She would do her job and, when the time came, leave without regret.

She hoped.

All she had to do now was let Jordan know she had succeeded. He had been sitting back, she knew, waiting for her to crawl back to him with her tail between her legs. And last night she had been so close to doing that, had never felt so miserable in her life.

The role of guardian angel sat oddly on Raff Quinlan's shoulders!

Dressing proved as difficult as she had thought it might, and by the time she had donned the thin woollen top and loose, flowered skirt the sweat stood out on her forehead and top lip, and she once again felt nauseous. But there was no telephone in her bedroom, and she had to find one. Besides, she was very curious about her surroundings, interested to see this estate Raff had talked about.

She stepped out of her bedroom into a long corridor, portraits adorning the walls, the resemblance of some of the subjects to Raff Quinlan pointing to their being his ancestors. So much for his casual dismissal the night before of his family name!

Arrogant-looking men and haughtily beautiful women seemed to follow her slow progress down the hallway, and every window she passed showed countryside, long fields, and magnificently tall trees. But there was an air of neglect about the immediate grounds, the gardens slightly overgrown, the driveway having tufts of grass growing among the gravel. Jane could see stables off to the right of the house, but the stalls looked empty of horses. Raff seemed to have been telling the truth about the lack of funds to spend on the estate, at least.

There were signs of the same lack of money in the house, too, with the bare spaces on walls where paintings other than those depicting ancestors had obviously once hung, but had probably been sold over the years in an effort to hang on to the estate at all. The carpets were old and worn too, although everywhere was obviously kept spotlessly clean by the efficient Mrs Howard.

It was a pity that such a beautiful old house couldn't be maintained in the way that it should have been, everything here in such sharp contrast to the luxury Jordan surrounded himself with.

Jordan.

He was the reason she had struggled down those stairs with her still painfully swollen ankle and stiff hip at all, her search for a telephone revealing one in the main hallway itself, her listening for Mrs Howard or Raff done almost furtively before she picked up the receiver and dialled.

The telephone rang and rang the other end. Jordan's housekeeper was finally the one to answer the call, and Jane remembered it was Henson's day off.

She asked for Jordan, knowing the call would be put through to his study at the back of the house where he couldn't be disturbed by street noise. She could even picture him as he sat behind his desk, his dark hair kept severely short, a perpetual frown between his grey-blue eyes. Poor Jordan, he never seemed to stop working.

'Yes?' he barked impatiently into the receiver, and Jane instantly knew she had been right about his being engrossed with work at his desk.

'It's Rhea-Jane,' she spoke briskly, and quickly, so that he shouldn't interrupt her. 'I'm well. I have a job. And I'm not coming home.' She quietly replaced the receiver before he could make any response.

She was trembling slightly as she straightened, committed now to working for Raff Quinlan. At least, for the moment . . .

CHAPTER THREE

RAFF hadn't been lying when he'd said he 'wasn't doing her any favours' by offering her the job of typing his correspondence; most of it was pretty boring, standard stuff to do with the estate, and there was a lot of it!

Jane had waited only two days after the accident before offering to start work on the typing, having spent most of that time alone, her meals served in her room, her wanderings down to the sitting-room in the evenings revealing only an empty room bare of any human warmth because its master wasn't present.

She knew she had to do something to break out of her rut when she had actually started seeking Raff's company!

She quickly discovered where he had been on those evenings she had sat alone wishing for even his abrasive presence, for replies to the dozens of letters that were piled up on a table in his study had been curtly dictated into the machine he had thrust into her hands on the morning she had tentatively approached the room Mrs Howard had told her was his study. There had been no surprise shown at her decision to accept his offer, just a brief explanation of where she could find everything she would need to start work before he'd excused himself to go off in search of a man he had fixing a fence out on the estate somewhere.

What had she expected? Gratitude? Pleasure? Relief? She would wait a long time for any of those emotions from Raff!

She hadn't seen any more of him after two days of typing until her fingers ached, unaccustomed as they were to moving on the typewriter keys. In fact, the only contact she had had with him had been a curt note stuck on one of the letters she had typed saying 'yield' was spelt 'ie' and not 'ei' as she had typed it! There wasn't a word said about the rest of the letters that had been neatly typed without *any* spelling mistakes.

But then, she was sure Raff didn't go around thanking Mrs Howard for keeping the family dinner service free of dust, or making sure the carpets were kept clean, either. She was an employee now, and she would do well to remember that!

To Jane's surprise Raff joined her in the dining-room for dinner that evening, and she couldn't help the thrill of pleasure just the sight of him gave her.

Ridiculous. She must be getting desperate for company if she could actually be pleased to see Raff Quinlan!

He didn't sit down, just stood across the table from her scowling down at her. 'I knew you were going to be trouble the moment I saw you,' he growled impatiently.

Jane sat back with a sigh of exasperation. 'What have I done now?'

He gave an irritated movement of his hand. 'My aunt and uncle have decided to come down for the weekend,' he announced curtly.

Jane knew a little more about the Quinlan family now, having had coffee with Mrs Howard in the mornings, although the other woman was most discreet, answering Jane's questions with the minimum of information without actually being rude. Jane knew that Raff was an only child, and he himself had told her both his parents were dead. His immediate family seemed to consist of his aunt Anita and her lawyer husband, and their three offspring.

This had to be the aunt and uncle Raff spoke of now. 'That will be nice,' she said slowly, for she could tell by Raff's expression that he thought it would be far from that. A thought suddenly occurred to her to make her feel anxious too. 'Does this mean you won't need me to do your typing any more?' Having kept a job for only two days had to be worse than having no job at all! How utterly humiliating!

'Anita isn't coming down here because she's interested in doing any work,' Raff instantly scorned.

'No?' Jane frowned.

'No,' he bit out impatiently. 'My dear aunt is only interested in seeing who the woman is I have staying here with me!'

'The woman you—— You mean me?' Jane gasped.

Raff gave her a pitying look. 'Are there any other women staying here?'

Of course there weren't, but Raff had given little indication he had even noticed she *was* here, so perhaps she could be excused for showing her surprise. Although Raff's derisive expression didn't seem to agree with her.

'I'm acting as your secretary,' she frowned; he had even let her advance to taking messages from the calls he received while he was out today—promotion indeed!

Raff's mouth twisted. 'You're also female.'

She arched mocking brows, her lips tilting challengingly. 'Am I?' she taunted. 'I didn't think you had noticed!'

Raff simply looked at her, the intimate knowledge he had of her body unclothed there in his gaze, and as he continued to look at her Jane felt the heat enter her cheeks.

Had she really thought, even briefly, that she could challenge this man? He would meet her challenge every time, and better it!

'What's the matter, Jane?' he said softly. 'Are you starting to miss having a man in your life?'

Her head went back at the insult, her defiance only wavering slightly as his gaze rested fiercely on the vividness of her hair. She put a hand up to the silken tresses self-consciously.

'What's the matter?'

He moved slowly, almost predatorily, coming around the table to stand so close to her she could feel the heat of his body through the black trousers and grey shirt he wore. His hand moved, almost against his will it seemed, the movement made jerkily as he gathered up a handful of the fiery hair.

'I should never have let you stay here,' he rasped, although he didn't seem to be speaking to her, but to himself.

The touch of his hand made her tremble, though she did her best to try to look unmoved by the intimacy.

'Red hair,' he muttered harshly. 'Damned red hair!' His hand clenched in her hair now, and in doing so it pulled her closer towards him.

Jane looked up at him with pained eyes, but he didn't seem to realise he was hurting her, staring at her hair as if it were about to catch fire in his hand.

She had noticed his reaction to her colouring in the hospital and then again the following morning in her bedroom upstairs. Oh, God, it would be just her luck if the wife who had walked out on him had been a redhead! It would certainly explain his behaviour now.

It didn't even begin to explain her own reaction towards him!

The man had been rude to her, insulted her in ways that no one else ever had, and yet she was more aware of him than she had been of any other man, could feel her pulse racing now, her breathing shallow, as if she was almost afraid to break the spell that held him captivated.

And yet, in a way, she knew he didn't even see her, that his thoughts were miles away...with some other woman, probably. Jane knew a sudden desperation to know more about the wife who had deserted him when he had apparently needed her the most.

But she was given no opportunity to voice her curiosity as Raff's mouth came crashing down on hers, arching her neck back painfully.

Her pulse leapt at the unexpectedness of his kiss, her first instinct to pull away from the anger that emanated from him. But then the anger seemed to leave him, the kiss suddenly slow and searching, his lips moving sensuously against hers.

She was lost, had never felt so helplessly out of her depth in her life.

It was only a kiss, she tried to convince herself.

But it was so much more.

She had never felt so totally weakened before, knew that if Raff decided to make love to her, here and now, she would be able to do nothing to stop him.

She looked up at him with darkened eyes as he at last raised his head from hers. 'Raff, I——'

'I wondered if——'

An embarrassed Mrs Howard stood in the doorway, her face colouring as she took in how close Raff and Jane were to each other.

'Erm—I'm sorry,' she attempted awkwardly. 'I only wanted to see—I'll come back later.' She turned to beat a hasty retreat.

'Mrs Howard,' Raff stopped her harshly. 'I was just on my way to see you anyway,' he announced, although it must have been obvious to all of them that that hadn't been his immediate plan.

Jane wasn't sure *what* his immediate plan had been! She would probably never know now, either.

Was she stupid? This man, despite having just kissed her, despised her too, and she was still living in his house only because she needed this job very badly, and for no other reason. To even imagine there could ever be anything between herself and Raff Quinlan was just asking for trouble.

When had she ever avoided trouble?

She dismissed this thought immediately. Raff Quinlan wasn't the man for her. Then why did her legs still feel weak and her arms ache to arch up about his neck and draw him back down to her?

'My aunt and uncle are coming down for the weekend,' he told the housekeeper abruptly. 'Could you make up a room for them?' He strode forcefully from the room without waiting for her reply.

Mrs Howard looked completely dazed. 'Miss Anita and her husband . . .?' She frowned. 'Why, I can't remember the last time they both——' She broke off, shaking her head, focusing slowly on Jane. 'I'm really sorry about just now, I didn't realise—I only wondered if Raff would be joining you for dinner,' she explained lamely.

Jane had come to like this woman very much over the last few days, and she respected her deeply for her unwavering loyalty to Raff and his family, guessing that the Quinlan family had become almost her own after her husband had died of a heart attack only a few years after they had been married.

She couldn't help but regret being partly to blame for the other woman's embarrassment now.

'It would appear not,' she shrugged ruefully. 'But I'll help you prepare the room for Raff's aunt after I've finished my meal if you would like me to?'

'Oh, I couldn't let you do that.' The older woman shook her head.

'Why not?' Jane instantly dismissed. 'I work here too, you know, and I'm well aware of the amount of work involved with clearing away after dinner.'

Mrs Howard seemed to run the household completely single-handedly, and while that was admirable she wasn't a youngster any more. And, in the circumstances, helping to prepare the bedroom seemed the least Jane could do; after all, if she weren't here she doubted Anita and her husband would be coming down to Quinlan House at all!

Anita Barnes turned out to be a female version of Raff when she arrived with her distinguished-looking lawyer husband the following afternoon—possessed of a regal elegance with her dark hair caught in a neat coil at her nape, the grey tailored dress suiting her tall slenderness.

She looked Jane up and down critically after Raff had introduced the two women, her eyes narrowing as she looked into Jane's face.

'Nice to meet you,' she greeted Jane off-handedly. 'You remind me of someone,' she accused without preamble.

Jane's eyes widened, feeling almost as if she had been attacked. 'Do I?' she returned with a politeness the other woman lacked. Anita Barnes, like her nephew, was someone who didn't suffer fools gladly. What a family! Jack Barnes seemed innocuous enough; he probably had to be with a wife like this!

'Hm.' The other woman still looked at her through narrowed lids. 'I'm not sure . . .'

'Anita, leave the poor girl alone,' Raff derided in a bored voice. 'Her name is Jane Smith, and she's a secretary. Leave it at that, will you?' he instructed tersely.

Neither statement was strictly accurate, but Jane wasn't about to argue with him.

'Hm, it will come to me soon, I'm sure.' Anita Barnes remained undiverted, although she turned her attention to her nephew now. 'I hope you don't mind, darling, but Bobby will be down some time before dinner.' The affectionate smile she gave completely transformed her face, making her look almost beautiful. 'The poor darling needed a little break from London; he's been working terribly hard.'

'Bobby's idea of working hard is getting up before ten o'clock in the morning,' Raff muttered as his aunt and uncle left the sitting-room to go upstairs and rest in their bedroom before dinner.

'Who is Bobby?' Jane asked, completely in the dark about his identity.

'Anita's oldest offspring,' Raff explained scornfully, 'and the apple of her eye. Bobby can do no wrong as far as Anita is concerned,' he added disparagingly.

Bobby Barnes. It sounded like a name of a football player, or maybe a boxer.

'He's an actor.' Raff instantly shattered that idea, his contempt for anything as frivolous as acting for a career evident in his expression. 'Unfortunately, Bobby is one of the ninety-five per cent of actors who are always out of work!'

'With a name like Bobby Barnes I'm not surprised!' Jane made a face.

'Hm, on the subject of names...' Raff's mood suddenly changed, his attention all centred on Jane now.

She was instantly wary, bracing her shoulders defensively. 'Yes?'

He nodded slowly. 'I telephoned the hotel you gave at the hospital as your last address——'

'You had no right!' she gasped, horrified that he had thought to do such a thing; it had never even occurred to her that he might do so. But she was living in his house, working for him; she had been a fool to think he would just accept her on face value alone. And now he had caught her completely off-guard!

'I had every right,' he rasped, moving closer to her. 'Do you know what they told me at the hotel?' he queried softly, his manner no less ominous for that.

That they had no Jane Smith registered the night she had claimed to be there...

She swallowed hard. 'No, what did they tell you?' she delayed, trying to think of some sensible remark she could possibly make to the question she knew had to be coming. There wasn't one!

Raff eyed her mockingly. 'That they aren't at liberty to tell me who may or may not have been guests at the hotel,' he drawled, dark brows arching as he watched the colour flood back into cheeks that had been pale with tension a moment ago. He gave a derisive inclination of his head. 'A pity, but there you are.'

Jane gave an inward sigh of relief, glaring up at Raff with resentful eyes. He had done that deliberately, had hoped to knock her off balance into possibly admitting something she otherwise wouldn't have done. Thank God she hadn't completely lost her nerve and done just that!

'Yes, isn't it?' she returned sweetly, completely insincere—as he was! 'I think I'll follow your aunt and uncle's example, and go up to my room for a rest before dinner,' she told him lightly, her head high as she crossed the room.

'Yes, do that,' Raff murmured from behind her. 'But, Jane...?'

She turned reluctantly, having no choice but to do so, although she made no verbal response.

'I'll continue searching and probing until I find out exactly who you are,' he warned softly, all mockery gone now. 'Just because I don't make an issue of it every time I see you, it doesn't mean I don't think about it.'

'I could be a criminal of some kind,' Jane challenged; she was shaken by his persistent interest, she couldn't deny it. She had been a fool to think even for a moment that he wouldn't pursue the subject.

'I don't think so,' he returned consideringly. 'But I hate mysteries,' he warned again.

Jane left the room more hurriedly than she would have liked to have done, stopping in the hallway to heave an exasperated sigh.

Raff could ruin everything for her with his 'searching and probing'...

Raff wasn't present when Jane entered the sitting-room later that evening; only Anita and Jack Barnes were there, the latter, as Jane had guessed, wearing a dinner-suit and snowy-white dinner-shirt. Jane had thought dinner with the Barneses present wouldn't be the casual affair she had been used to, which was why she had put on the royal blue cocktail dress, its design simple, but comfortable to wear on her still bruised body, the bodice fitted, the skirt flowing silkily about her shapely legs.

Anita Barnes had swapped one tailored dress for another—black this time, but just as expensively cut.

Bobby Barnes didn't seem to have put in an appearance yet, unless he too was still changing for dinner.

Jane couldn't help feeling curious about how Raff would look in a dinner-suit. Devastatingly attractive, she decided defeatedly. She was becoming altogether too interested in Raff Quinlan, the memory of the kiss they had shared the evening before having kept her awake long into the night. It had been no casual kiss, and had seemed almost against Raff's will. Her lips still tingled from the touch of his, and she looked about her guiltily as she knew her conflicting emotions must have shown in her face. Fortunately Anita Barnes didn't consider she had to make polite conversation with the 'hired help', and her attention was centred on her husband as she talked to him in her imperious voice. Jane took the opportunity to get her wandering thoughts firmly under control.

'Miss Jane Smith, I presume?'

She swung round at the sound of that mocking voice, a voice that was more than vaguely familiar, her breath catching in her throat as she looked up at the dark-haired young man with his classical good looks and laughing blue eyes.

Robert Barnstable!

And he knew damn well she wasn't 'Miss Jane Smith' at all!

CHAPTER FOUR

JANE closed her eyes, willing him to disappear, but he was still standing mockingly in front of her when she opened them again.

She had been so deep in thought she hadn't been aware of anyone having entered the room, but now she looked up at Robert with disbelieving eyes. Why *him*? Was nothing going to go right for her?

'Bobby Barnes, I presume?' she returned softly, although inside she was quietly panicking.

For, by a process of elimination, in the same way he had probably realised she was 'Jane Smith', she knew this had to be Raff's cousin Bobby.

It was just her luck that 'Bobby' had turned out to be one of the group of young actors she knew well in town.

Unfortunately she hadn't known Robert well enough to realise Barnstable was a stage-name!

It *was* just her luck.

He grinned down at her, wickedly good-looking, wearing his dinner-suit with a natural elegance. But then he did have natural grace and charm, especially charm. She had been out to dinner with him herself at least once, and had found him very good

64

company, not at all inclined to want to talk about himself all evening, the way some actors were.

But she would never, in a million years, have guessed that he and Raff were cousins!

'If you ever tell any of that crowd in London that my family call me Bobby...!' He groaned at the embarrassment of it.

Jane didn't return his smile, looking up at him intently. 'I'm more concerned with whether or not you intend telling your family, especially Raff, what the crowd in London call me!'

'Ah,' he said more soberly. 'Well, I must admit to being slightly baffled by what you're doing here?'

She shrugged. 'Raff seems to think I could be on the look-out for a rich protector.'

Robert's splutter of laughter caused his parents to look at them curiously, Anita Barnes instantly displeased to see her son talking to Jane at all, let alone actually enjoying her company.

It was also the moment Raff chose to enter the room, his steady gaze narrowing on them as they stood so close together across the room from him.

As Jane had rightly surmised, he wore his dinner-suit and snowy-white shirt with complete disregard for their formality, his hair curling damply over the collar of the latter, revealing that he had recently taken a shower.

'Yes, well, he would, wouldn't he?' Robert remarked drily, meeting the other man's gaze challengingly. 'My cousin's estimation of women isn't very high. Mind you, with an ex-wife like Celia that isn't surprising,' he grimaced.

Celia. At last Jane knew Raff's wife's name. Not that it did any good to know it, it only made her seem more real, more someone who had meant something in his life. And, somehow, that was painful to even think of.

'Maybe I remind Raff of her?' she suggested, hoping Robert wouldn't pick up on the intense curiosity she had to know more about the other woman, to try to understand what sort of woman it was that had made Raff as cynical as he was.

'You?' Robert frowned down at her. 'No.' He shook his head. 'Celia was tall and willowy.'

And she was short and skinny! 'I thought possibly my hair...?' She curled one of the flowing strands around her fingers, Raff's attention having been momentarily claimed by his uncle, who seemed completely unaware of Raff's interest in Jane and his son. Or his wife's!

'Your hair?' Robert looked even more puzzled now. 'What about your hair?' His frown deepened.

'I thought—— Wasn't Celia a redhead?' It was Jane's turn to look unsure now.

Robert laughed softly. 'Blonde, brunette, black, every colour you can think of, but I don't think she was ever—— Wait a minute.' He paused thoughtfully. 'Yes, I think she may have been a redhead when she and Raff first got married. Hm, I'm almost sure she was.' His brow cleared. 'But it wasn't for long,' he dismissed. 'Celia seemed to change the colour of her hair to match the clothes she wore!' he told Jane ruefully.

But she had been a redhead when Raff first married her...

It was one explanation for the way he seemed to dislike the colour of her hair, the way it seemed to make him more angry with her. But he couldn't blame every other woman with red hair for the way his initially red-haired wife had let him down!

She shrugged. 'Maybe it's just me he distrusts,' she sighed. 'He gives the impression no man is safe with me.'

'I should be so lucky!' Robert looked at her admiringly.

He had never made any secret of the fact that he found her attractive, and Jane knew that tonight she looked better than she had done for some days, the pallor from her accident having faded, made more so by the application of a light make-up, her blue dress flowing silkily over her body, her hair like a bright, shimmering flame as it cascaded down over her bare shoulders.

Raff was looking at her again now, but if *he* found her in the least appealing he didn't show it, glaring at her coldly while remaining in conversation with his aunt.

Looking at the two men, it was clear which one was the more obviously attractive, and yet, despite all Robert's charm and good looks, Jane knew that of the two she was more attracted to Raff.

Strange . . . until recently she had never thought of herself as a masochist!

'I believe we're about to go in to dinner now that my dear cousin has finally decided to join us,' Robert said drily. 'You still haven't enlightened me as to what "Jane Smith" is doing here acting as Raff's secretary, so I'll have to get back to you again later. You know, Raff might change his attitude a little if he knew who you really are,' he mused.

Jane eyed him sceptically. 'Do you really think so?' She thought of the life she had previously led, and knew it wouldn't find favour in Raff's eyes at all.

'Maybe not,' Robert acknowledged with a grimace. 'Actually,' he added conspiratorially, 'I'm more than a little curious to find out how Jordan feels about your working here?'

'It must be obvious he has no idea.' Jane frowned her irritation.

'Hence "Jane Smith", I suppose?' Robert nodded. 'Hm, I'm sure Jordan would be very interested to learn of your whereabouts.'

'Don't even think about——'

'Have to go, Rhea—er—I mean, Jane.' Robert grimaced. 'Better not make a mistake like that again, had I? I'll talk to you again later,' he promised.

'Oh, but——'

'My mother is waiting impatiently for me to escort her in to dinner.' He patted Jane's arm reassuringly in a distracted way, his attention already transferred to his mother as she glared at him disapprovingly from across the room, obviously furious at the amount of time he had spent talking to Jane.

She didn't envy him his mother's wrath, sure that Anita Barnes was a force to be reckoned with when angry, if she was anything like her nephew; and Jane felt sure, even on so brief an acquaintance, that that woman could be very like him. Even being 'the apple of his mother's eye' wouldn't save Robert from her displeasure, Jane was certain.

As the only other female in the room Jane should really have been escorted in to dinner by Jack Barnes, but he seemed to be taking his cue from his wife, obviously knowing better than to anger her any further where Jane was concerned, strolling in to the dining-room at his wife's other side.

There was an awkward silence as Jane and Raff realised they had no choice but to go in to dinner together.

And Raff looked far from pleased about it!

Maybe she shouldn't have joined them for dinner at all this evening; she was, after all, only an employee, and Anita Barnes didn't give the impression she usually ate with the 'hired hands'.

But Raff should have told her earlier if that was the case; she couldn't not go into dinner with the family now!

Raff made no effort to offer her his arm. 'What do you think you're doing?' he rasped.

She blinked up at him. 'I——'

'Stay away from my little cousin,' he warned harshly.

She drew in a sharply angry breath. 'He came over and started talking to *me*,' she bit out indignantly. 'What was I supposed to do, be rude to him?' She glared up at Raff. 'I suppose then I would have been reprimanded for *that*,' she added impatiently. 'I can't seem to win with you!'

With that, she turned on her heel and walked into the dining-room without him, uncaring of how odd that must look.

Robert raised questioning brows at her flushed cheeks and glittering eyes.

'Are you working at the moment?' she asked him as she took her seat at the table down the opposite end to Raff, as he pulled his own chair out and sat down with the minimum of movement, his body stiff with anger. 'Raff tells me you're an actor,' she smiled encouragingly at Robert, determined not to be completely unnerved by Raff's contemptuous attitude.

Robert nodded, more than happy to pour fuel on the tension he sensed between Jane and Raff. 'I'm rehearsing a play,' he said with satisfaction.

'That must be fascinating,' she prompted, studiously ignoring Raff, although she knew his angry gaze was still on her.

Robert gave her a look that told her he knew exactly what was going on, and he was more than willing to help her annoy Raff. In fact, anyone listening to him over the next couple of hours could be forgiven for believing that goading Raff was what Robert lived for!

Jane could perfectly understand why that was— the two men being complete opposites, Raff taking life so seriously, Robert treating everything as if it were a game.

Raff's manner got frostier and frostier, his eyes colder and colder, as the evening wore on.

Anita Barnes didn't look too thrilled by her son's apparent interest in her nephew's secretary either, any comments she made to Jane being waspish, to say the least.

By the coffee stage of the meal Jane just wanted to escape from the situation she had helped to create because of her annoyance with Raff. Anita Barnes was just watching her with narrowed eyes now, and Raff himself looked ready to commit murder—with Jane as his obvious victim!

'You know, Raff,' Anita Barnes spoke slowly, her head tilted thoughtfully as she looked at Jane, 'I've finally remembered who your secretary reminds me of. I knew it would come to me if I just gave myself a little time,' she added with satisfaction.

'Yes?' Raff sat stiffly erect in his chair.

'Yes,' his aunt turned to him with narrowed eyes. 'It was that woman your father was involved with.'

Raff's mouth tightened. 'I'm sorry, I don't know what you mean,' he bit out tersely.

Neither did Jane; as far as she was aware Raff's parents had been together when they died in the plane crash and, if that were so, how could Raff possibly know any woman his father had been involved with previous to his marriage? Raff wouldn't even have been born!

She watched the aunt and nephew curiously, Raff seeming not at all pleased with the turn the conversation had taken.

'Of course you do,' Anita said dismissively. 'She was your nanny at the time.' She turned to her husband. 'You remember her, Jack,' she encouraged. 'What was her name? I'm surprised you don't remember it, Raff; you were so very fond of her. I remember how heart-broken you were when she left so suddenly,' she derided.

'I——'

'It was Diana,' Raff put in softly. 'And I don't care to have personal family business discussed just now,' he warned his aunt coldly.

Because of Jane's presence, she knew. But he needn't have worried; she wasn't at all interested in any skeletons in this family's closet. Except that the conversation had set off little alarm bells in her own mind; her mother had been a nanny before she'd married her father, and her first name was Diana...

But it had to be a coincidence. Good grief, the Princess of Wales herself was named Diana, and she had worked with children before her marriage too!

Nevertheless, it was slightly unsettling...

'Busy?'

Jane looked up at Robert as he stood framed in the doorway of the small sitting-room where she sat.

And it must have been obvious, as she sat on this small chintz-covered sofa, idly flicking through a magazine she had no real interest in, that she wasn't doing anything in the least important!

She put the magazine down on the seat beside her. 'Extremely,' she drawled sarcastically.

He grinned down at her as he entered the room. 'That's what I thought.'

She grimaced. 'Actually, I am busy—staying out of everyone's way!'

She had made her excuses as soon as she possibly could once the meal had finished the previous evening, and had managed to avoid any further contact with the family today by going for a walk as soon as she'd got up, and taking some sandwiches with her so that she didn't have to join the family for another tension-filled meal.

Unfortunately the Barneses' BMW and Robert's more flamboyant sports car were still parked in the driveway next to Raff's old-style Jaguar when she'd returned late in the afternoon, and so she had taken refuge in this small sitting-room that was rarely used. Robert must have actually been looking for her to have found her in here.

'The parents have just departed,' he told her with a grin, perching on the wooden arm of one of the chairs that matched the chintz sofa.

Jane wasn't at all surprised that the couple hadn't felt it necessary to actually say their goodbyes to her; she was only an employee, after all.

'My mother having settled herself you aren't after the family silver,' Robert continued mockingly, dressed casually today in denims and a loose white cotton top.

'After the——?' Jane spluttered indignantly. 'Surely if that were what I was after I would have taken it and run by now?' As far as she was aware the family didn't *have* any silver!

'Oh, I didn't mean silver of the precious metal kind...' Robert arched meaningful brows.

'Then what——?' She broke off, her eyes widening as she thought Robert's meaning was becoming clear. 'You don't mean *Raff*?' She was incredulous at the mere idea of it.

Robert nodded. 'Mother has it in mind for Raff to remain unmarried, and for me to one day inherit all this.' He waved his arms about pointedly.

But could Anita and her family, even if this preposterous idea were true, not see the financial difficulties the estate was in, and just how little there would be for Robert to inherit as Raff's heir? Although the other couple were obviously rich in their own right, so perhaps this didn't worry them unduly. Jane had no doubt that even if the Barneses were in a financial position to help him, Raff would never ask them for it; he was a proud man, determined to make it—or not, whichever it turned out to be!—on his own merits.

'One look at Raff and I together, and your mother knew I was no danger to her aspirations,' Jane said drily.

Robert grinned. 'Raff has always been blind where women are concerned.'

She felt a little uncomfortable discussing him in this way—even with Robert, who had been something of a personal friend in London.

'Maybe he has good reason to be,' she dismissed, thinking of his broken marriage.

'Maybe,' his cousin acknowledged uninterestedly. 'His father wasn't too lucky in love either. None of the male members of this family seem to have been, now that I come to think of it.' He frowned.

'But Raff's parents must have been married over thirty years.' She was intrigued in spite of herself at the mention of Raff's father twice in as many days.

'Married, yes,' Robert said drily. 'Happily, no. Aunt Helen, Raff's mother, was something of a bitch. She and Celia were the best of friends,' he added, as if that said it all.

And maybe it did. But how sad that both the Quinlan men, father and son, had been so unhappy in their marriages.

But it still left the question of the woman, Diana, whom *she* reminded Anita Barnes of.

'Who was Diana?' she asked curiously.

Robert shrugged. 'I don't really know. Before my time, I'm afraid. I didn't actually come here to talk about Raff or the rest of the happy family,' he asserted. 'I'm still agog to know what you're doing here playing at secretaries?' he taunted.

'I'm not playing at it,' she protested indignantly. 'I'll admit I'm not very good at it, but I work fast enough for Raff, which is what matters. And it *is* a job,' she shrugged.

'But why do you need one?' He still looked puzzled.

As well he might. Much as she disliked having to do it, she knew that nothing less than the complete truth would appease Robert. And maybe she owed him that much for keeping quiet what he knew about her.

She looked at him warningly. 'This is in the strictest confidence.'

He sat forward on the arm of the chair. 'I'm all ears,' he encouraged confidingly.

Jane gave him a censorious glare. 'This isn't funny, Robert.'

He held up his hands defensively. 'I'm not laughing.'

'You aren't taking it seriously, either.' Jane stood up impatiently, striding over to the window, staring out at the rolling hills while she tried to collect her thoughts together. Finally she turned back to him.

'In just under three months' time I shall be twenty-one,' she began slowly. 'If by that time I have managed to stay in useful employment—a job where I actually earn a wage rather than the charity work I have been involved in so far—I inherit the money my father left for me.' She gave a grimace of disgust at her father's obvious lack of trust in her.

She had never had an easy relationship with her father, and had been away at finishing-school in Switzerland when he had died just over two years ago. She had come back to England to take over running the houses he had all over the world, and become so caught up with that that it had been increasingly difficult for her to do anything else, although charity work had also featured largely in her busy life.

But Jordan had known of the stipulation in her father's will if she was to inherit the full fortune which had been left to her; indeed he was one of the trustees who would decide whether or not she should inherit.

'Jordan doesn't believe I can do it,' she added hardly.

'It's incredible!' Robert breathed softly. 'It's like something out of a Victorian novel.'

Jane sighed. 'My father had little belief in women's capabilities.'

'Your mother...?'

'Died when I was born,' she rasped sharply. 'But you see why I need this job so badly?' She frowned. 'At the moment I'm totally dependent on Jordan except for my allowance, and I want more than anything to be free of the financial hold he has over me.'

Robert looked troubled. 'I had no idea...'

'No one does,' she sighed. 'And I would much rather it stayed that way.'

'It's awful for you,' he agreed. 'But I've always thought Jordan was a decent sort, even if he can seem a little unapproachable at times.'

'Oh, Jordan is—well, he's just Jordan,' Jane shrugged. 'A law unto himself most of the time,' she accepted ruefully. 'But I—I want to do something else with my life other than be the social butterfly everyone seems to think I am. I'd like to start up a business of my own.'

The enthusiasm she had kept firmly in check bubbled to the surface, and her eyes glowed. 'Despite what Jordan might think to the contrary,' she said drily, 'I've discovered over the last weeks that I am qualified to do something. As a social hostess

I have no rivals,' she grinned. 'With the money from my inheritance I could set up an agency. There must be dozens of people who would value my help and advice for their social functions.'

'Oh, dozens,' Robert echoed wryly.

She looked at him sharply. 'You don't think so?' she said uncertainly.

It was an idea that had been formulating in her mind over the last few days, none of the plans concrete yet, the idea just slowly fermenting and growing. Why not? She was more than qualified, and it would be something she had always wanted—to be able to run her own business, to be an independent woman.

He shrugged. 'If anyone can make it work I'm sure you can. It seems a pity you have to put up with grim old Raff to get your inheritance, though. Although,' he added consideringly, 'I don't suppose he's any grimmer than Jordan. Why hasn't he caused an uproar about your just taking off like that?' Robert mused.

'Pride,' she answered without hesitation. Jordan would never admit he wasn't in complete control, of any situation. 'Besides, what could he really tell anyone? I've over eighteen, and there is no reason to presume I'm actually missing.'

'But you used the name "Jane Smith" just to be on the safe side?' Robert taunted.

Her cheeks were flushed at the gibe. 'How do you think Raff would have reacted if I had used my full name?' she said defensively.

'Hm,' Robert nodded. 'I see your point.'

'Don't think it wasn't tried and tested,' Jane added ruefully. 'I went after a dozen or so jobs in town before I got this one, and at the ones where I used my full name the reaction was always the same: what did I want a job for at all? Raff already distrusts me enough without that added complication.'

'Because you're female,' Robert acknowledged matter-of-factly.

'Possibly.' Although Jane still wasn't a hundred per cent certain about that, and wondered if her similarity to this woman, Diana, who had been in his father's life might have something to do with it. She would probably never know.

'Hm, well, I don't envy you explaining things to Jordan when you finally resurface. But I take it from all this you don't want me to say hello to him for you?' he teased with a grin.

'Over your dead body!' She could just imagine the embarrassing scene that would ensue if Jordan were to come here in search of her!

Robert quirked dark brows. 'What's it worth?'

'Mandy Padbury,' she returned instantly, reminding him of an embarrassing relationship she was sure he wouldn't want his family, now that she had met them, to know about!

'Unfair!' he grimaced in defeat.

They laughed softly together, but Jane's humour faded as soon as Robert had gone; she still had Raff to face after last night . . .

CHAPTER FIVE

WHAT was that strange noise?

It wasn't a loud noise, just persistent, despite being irregular. Or maybe it seemed persistent because it was irregular? It was like waiting for the dripping of a tap, listening for the sound of the next tapping noise.

It hadn't woken Jane; she hadn't been to sleep yet. The meeting with Raff that she had dreaded still hadn't taken place. Immediately after his guests had all left he'd gone out on estate business, and Jane had long been in her bedroom when she'd heard the sound of his car returning.

Perhaps it hadn't been estate business at all? Maybe his family were all wrong about him, and he had a girlfriend somewhere in the district? Although from the little she had come to know of him over the last few days she didn't think he was the type of man to kiss one woman—no matter how provoked he had felt at the time!—while having a relationship with another. And he had most definitely kissed her!

It was while she was in the library looking for a book to read because she couldn't sleep that she had first heard those faint tap-tapping noises.

Maybe it was burglars, trying to break the glass in a window without actually rousing the household? She wouldn't have heard the noise herself if she hadn't already been downstairs.

She tentatively followed the sound of the tapping noises, her sky-coloured nightgown and wrap floating silkily about her ankles as she crept along soundlessly in the matching coloured mules.

The sound seemed to be coming from inside Raff's study, the door being slightly ajar, a light visible inside, despite it being almost two o'clock in the morning.

Who could be in there this time of night? Raff had gone to bed hours ago. At least, she had presumed he had gone to bed...

Endearing was not a word she had ever thought to associate with that arrogantly autocratic man, and yet it was the only word she could use to describe seeing a thirty-seven year old man wrestling with the keys of a typewriter as if it were almost a foreign object. But it probably was to him!

He had obviously been bent over his task for some time now, his brow furrowed into a frown of deep concentration, the sheet of paper inside the typewriter only half covered with print. And at the speed he was typing it must have taken him hours to do. No wonder he appreciated her slow but accurate efforts if this was the best he could do!

But what was he doing typing for at all? That was what she was still here for. But perhaps he didn't want her to see what he was typing. The question now was, should she let him know of her presence, or just sneak away to her bedroom unseen?

Even as she posed the question to herself Raff's head rose and he looked across the room at her.

He didn't actually seem to see her standing there for several seconds, but blinked suddenly, slowly focusing on her as his mind cleared slightly. As he did so, the harshness entered his eyes. 'What are you doing down here?' he rasped.

She had never met a man who could make her feel so uncomfortable!

But this scene—the desk scattered with business papers in the middle of the night, and even the furrowed brow of the man behind the desk—was an all too familiar sight to her.

'Can I get you some coffee and buttered toast?' she offered, having no idea whether he had eaten dinner while he was out or not. But she had learnt from experience that coffee and toast this time of night usually had the effect of reviving Jordan.

Raff sat back in his chair. 'You shouldn't be awake this time of night.' He ignored her offer.

'I couldn't sleep,' she explained.

He frowned, looking at her critically. 'Are you in pain?'

Except for the odd twinge from her ankle and a slight soreness to her hip her injuries no longer troubled her. They certainly didn't keep her awake at night. Thoughts of this man managed to do that quite successfully!

'I ache sometimes,' she admitted truthfully. 'But there's no real pain any more,' she assured him, noticing that Raff instantly looked relieved.

'Actually, I was looking for a book in the library when I heard you typing,' she calmly answered his earlier accusatory question. 'Although I didn't realise it was typing at the time; I thought it might have been a burglar,' she ruefully admitted her folly.

Raff shook his head. 'But you came looking for the source of the noise anyway?' he derided drily. 'You seem to be making a habit of walking into trouble because you don't practise caution.'

'I wouldn't have tackled the burglar myself!' she returned heatedly.

'He would have been wasting his time anyway.' Raff gave a weary smile. 'There's nothing left in the house worth stealing.'

'Coffee and toast,' Jane decided firmly, knowing from nights like this with Jordan that when he was hungry and over-tired his defences were down.

Raff gave her a scathing look. 'You don't look as if you've ever done more than simply appear decorous in that outfit. Are you sure you know where the kitchen is?' he scorned.

She held her tongue with effort, smiling tightly before leaving the room; she hadn't expected her offer would sweeten his temper.

It was just as well, because she would have been disappointed!

She not only knew where the kitchen was in this huge house, she also knew where everything was kept in it. It took her very little time to make a pot of coffee and a plate of hot buttered toast.

She could hear Raff typing determinedly again as she approached his study in the still quietness of the rest of the house. But, for all his derision of her, he got up quickly enough when she entered the room, and made a space for the tray on top of the desk.

'Black for me,' he requested gruffly as she poured the coffee into two mugs. Even these seemed to have come as a surprise to him, as if he expected her to drink coffee out of nothing but the best china cups.

But somehow coffee tasted better in mugs at this time of night. Raff obviously thought so too, downing the strong brew with obvious pleasure, and eating several of the half-slices of toast, too.

He looked better already; the lines of strain eased about his mouth, slight colour came back in his cheeks, making her doubt again that he had actually had any dinner earlier. He was a big man, and not eating proper meals couldn't be good for him. Neither could working in here until this time—not when she knew he was up and about the estate by seven o'clock most mornings.

'Can't that wait until tomorrow?' she prompted gently, nodding towards the half finished type-written sheet.

He groaned at the reminder of the typing he had been doing when she'd entered the room. 'As I told you when I asked you to stay on here and help with my correspondence, I just don't have the time to do this during the day.'

'As you've just pointed out, I thought that was what I was here for.' Jane frowned.

He shook his head. 'This file is too...confidential for me to trust it to anyone else,' he said.

And she couldn't be trusted was what he didn't say. He didn't even know her real name yet—although he would continue to work on it!

'Who could I tell, Raff?' she scorned.

He shrugged, watching her through narrowed eyes. 'You tell me.'

She sighed. 'All right, struggle on alone, if that's what you want!' She stood up to leave.

'You're very touchy tonight,' Raff drawled mockingly. 'Have some toast.' He pushed the plate towards her. 'It's just about the best toast anyone has ever made for me,' he added gruffly. 'Not too much butter, but not too little either. And perfectly melted into the toast.'

As olive branches went it could use a little work, but coming from Raff Quinlan she knew she wouldn't get any more than that.

As for the perfect toast, that had come after much practice on Jordan; he was probably as much a taskmaster as Raff was. He could be so stuffy at times, although his fussiness over how his toast was buttered seemed to have actually paid off for her.

The two men were alike, not only in their looks, but their manner was very similar too. Although perhaps Raff had a little more humour to him than Jordan; Jordan would never have let 'little Jane Smith' stay on in his home when he was almost certain that wasn't her real name. He wouldn't see it as the challenge Raff obviously did.

Jane took half a slice of the toast—not really because she was hungry, but more out of an effort to show she wasn't going to bear a grudge because he didn't trust her enough to let her do some very private typing for him; there would be no point in such childish sulks.

'Just like mother used to make,' she returned lightly.

Raff's mouth twisted. 'I doubt my mother ever made me toast,' he said drily.

'No boiled eggs and toast soldiers when you were ill?' she teased, almost able to imagine him as a little boy, all dark tousled hair and big grey eyes. He would have been adorable.

'No,' he laughed derisively.

'Mine neither,' Jane said wistfully. 'My mother died when I was born,' she explained at his questioning look.

He frowned. 'I'm sorry.' He obviously genuinely meant the emotion, and wasn't just paying polite lip-service.

'I'm not so sure *she* was.'

Jane wasn't even looking at Raff now, talking almost to herself as she became lost in memories.

'My parents' marriage was reputedly very rocky, and had been for some years. I was apparently a last-ditch attempt on their part to bridge the ever-widening rift. I don't think my father ever forgave me for the fact that my mother died having me and left that particular riddle undone. He was a very methodical man,' she added without bitterness, her voice flat now.

Jane didn't realise that she had revealed in those few brief sentences all the lonely years of her childhood when she had first tried to win her father's love by being so good he couldn't help but be proud of her, and when that failed becoming an out-and-out rebel so that he at least had to notice her!

He had noticed her all right, instantly placing her in a boarding-school—which she had promptly got herself expelled from. And then another boarding-school. And another. All of her school life had been spent going from one boarding-school to another because she was so rebellious, until at last she was old enough to leave.

Only her father hadn't even wanted her back home then, arranging for her to go to Switzerland to a finishing-school. Being a rebel and getting herself noticed had become such a part of her life by then that she had continued to be uncooperative until her father had died two years ago.

Even as she'd stood at his graveside watching them lower his coffin into the ground she had wondered if there had been *anything* she could have done to make him love her? The answer had been a resounding no; she had merely been a means to an end as far as her father was concerned—one that was no longer necessary with the death of her mother. She had simply been a reminder that he didn't even want in his sight.

And she had never before talked to anyone about—or even hinted at—the rejection she had felt from her father from birth.

She looked dazedly across the desk at Raff, wondering why it should be this man she allowed to see her pain beneath the veneer of sophistication?

He seemed to be aware of her sudden uncertainty, her vulnerability from what she had unwittingly revealed.

'My own parents' marriage wasn't any recommendation either,' he admitted ruefully. 'They lived apart for a lot of my early childhood, and I only have sketchy memories of my mother being involved in my life after that.' He grimaced. 'Hence my aunt's indiscreet remark yesterday about my father's involvement with another woman.'

Diana. The nanny. *Raff's* nanny.

Jane swallowed hard. 'Did you like her? This other woman? Diana, wasn't it? Your aunt said she looked after you——' she shrugged as his mouth suddenly became tight '—that I reminded her of this woman...'

'Rubbish,' he bit out harshly. 'Oh, I'll grant you there's a surface similarity in the colouring and your build, but that's all it is, a similarity!'

'Mrs Howard said I reminded *her* of someone too the first morning we met,' Jane remembered slowly. She was sure now that this woman Diana had to be the one the housekeeper had meant that morning. And after realising Raff had once been married *she* had assumed it had been Celia she reminded everyone of.

Diana. A nanny.

Her mother?

The only way she could actually be sure would be to reveal her own identity and ask Raff outright if Diana's surname had been Holmes. And she wasn't ready to give up her job here yet.

Besides, this Diana, the other Diana—if it had been another Diana!—had been involved with Raff's father. It couldn't have been her mother.

Could it...?

'I told you, a surface similarity,' Raff dismissed again. 'If it weren't for your hair no one would even think twice about it.'

In all of the photographs of her mother she had seen, her hair had been as long and red as Jane's own ...

'Look, it's late now, Jane.' Raff stood up to come round to her side of the desk. 'We're both tired, and need some sleep.'

She wasn't sure she would be able to sleep after this!

Raff put up a hand to the paleness of her cheek, shaking his head reprovingly as she swayed slightly.

'You shouldn't be up this late,' he murmured, swinging her up into his arms. 'You were very badly bruised only a few days ago. Don't struggle,' he warned softly when Jane began to squirm as he carried her out of the room and up the wide staircase.

He carried her with ease, but he was too close, his warmth enveloping her, her arms clinging about his neck.

He made her feel small, and feminine, and utterly defenceless.

She began to struggle again as they entered her bedroom.

'Don't——' His chiding reprimand broke off abruptly as he looked down at her, grey eyes looking deeply into dark blue. 'Jane!' He gave a strangulated groan as he lowered his lips to hers.

Jane slid slowly down the length of his body as he lowered her feet to the floor, the kiss seeming to go on forever, and yet it wasn't enough for either of them.

Their mouths moved together hungrily, Jane giving a husky gasp of pleasure as one of Raff's hands moved to cup her breast, its tip straining forward, hardened with longing.

And her ache was of a different kind now; Raff's thighs moulded against her own, telling her of his need too.

Raff's hands cupped either side of her face now as he rested his forehead on hers, his breathing ragged. 'I'm supposed to be taking care of you, not——'

He shook his head with self-disgust, straightening. 'Put this down to the lateness of the hour,' he advised harshly. 'It couldn't be anything else,' he muttered as he abruptly left the room.

Jane sat down heavily on the bed, her eyes huge blue pools of vulnerability.

'Telephone?' She frowned up at Mrs Howard the following morning as she sat bent over the desk she worked on, doing her best not to even think about what had happened the previous evening. As she was sure Raff was!

She sensed the other woman's interest in the fact that this was the first private telephone call Jane had received since she had come here almost a week ago.

And who could blame her?

'For me?' Jane blinked her surprise. 'Are you sure?'

She wasn't sure of anything herself any more, and didn't see why anyone else should be!

'Of course I'm sure!' The housekeeper was slightly put out that Jane should doubt her word.

'Thank you,' Jane accepted heavily, getting slowly to her feet to go and take the call in the hallway.

Robert—it had to be; he was the only one who knew she was here. Well, the only person who would know to ask for 'Jane Smith'!

She only hoped he wasn't about to make a nuisance of himself because of that. She didn't need him popping in and out of her life—not now. She already had too many other complications to deal with.

Consequently, when she lifted up the receiver she wasn't feeling kindly disposed to Robert's being a disruptive presence in her already turbulent life. 'Yes?' she prompted tersely.

'It's Jordan,' came the harshly unexpected reply. 'I'm well, too—in the circumstances! But I want to know more about this job of yours. I'll be waiting for you in our favourite restaurant tomorrow at one o'clock. Be there.'

The receiver was put down at the other end with a decisive click.

Jane was too stunned to even move for several minutes.

She had been partly right, for it had to have been Robert who'd told Jordan of her whereabouts!

And if she didn't meet Jordan tomorrow for lunch as he had instructed she knew he was capable of coming here instead.

Which would cause all sorts of problems.

Damn Robert!

CHAPTER SIX

'*Moi?*' Robert questioned with exaggerated innocence when Jane telephoned him to tell him exactly
what she thought of his betrayal.

'Mandy wasn't enough of a deterrent, hm?' Jane
said coolly.

'It wasn't that,' he wheedled, all bravado gone.
'Of all things to happen to me, when I got back to
town on Sunday night I bumped straight into
Jordan. He was in the foulest temper imaginable,
and I knew that if he ever found out I had known
where you were and hadn't told him...! Put
yourself in my place, Rhea,' he pleaded.

Jane could do that all too easily; Jordan could
be formidable. But it didn't make her situation here
any easier. Because of Robert she now had to try
to get tomorrow off so that she could go into town
and meet Jordan.

She had to accept that there was little more she
could say to Robert on the subject, although she
left him in no doubt about how annoyed she was
with him.

It was asking Raff for the day off that was going
to be so difficult; she hadn't even worked for him
a full week yet.

He had fallen back into the habit of not joining her for dinner since the departure of his aunt and uncle, and so she had no choice but to seek him out in his study after she had finished her own meal. There was a tray with empty plates put to one side of his desk to show that he had at least eaten.

But he looked more tired than ever tonight, and there was a wary look on his face as he glanced up and saw her.

Jane knew the reason for that wariness, knew he was unsure how they were supposed to behave towards each other after last night.

For a man like Raff the emotion must be galling!

Well, if he thought she had assumed anything after their kisses the previous night he was mistaken; she didn't think it would ever pay to assume anything where this man was concerned.

'I just brought coffee for us both tonight.' She held up the two cups as she entered the room.

'Thanks,' he accepted abruptly, taking one of the cups before sitting down again behind the desk.

Jane hesitated, and then sat down in the chair opposite him. He didn't have the typewriter on the desk in front of him tonight, just long, hand-written pages.

Raff saw her gaze on them. 'I—er—decided to write the report out again by hand, and thought I would accept your offer of last night.'

God, how that cost him!

'Why?' she prompted softly.

He shrugged. 'The report is pretty urgent,' he bit out curtly, obviously hating having to change his mind like this after what he had said to her yesterday. 'I'd like you to start work on it as soon as possible.'

'Of course,' she nodded. 'I'll start typing it straight away if you have some of it already completed?'

He gave a slight smile. 'There's no need to do that, tomorrow will do.'

Now it was her turn to look uncertain. 'I—er—I know this might seem a bit cheeky, but I wondered if I could have tomorrow off?' The last came out in a rush, and she looked at him ruefully.

'Why?' he returned, as she had seconds earlier, his eyes narrowed searchingly on her flushed face.

'I—need to go into London for the day,' she explained with a grimace of reluctance. But she couldn't just swan off for the day without asking Raff. She may not be used to being employed by someone, but she did at least know that!

'Your days off are Saturday and Sunday,' Raff told her harshly.

'I'll work on Saturday instead of tomorrow to make up for it,' she promised.

He gave a deep sigh, sitting back in his chair. 'I know I don't have the right to interfere in your life——'

'No, you don't,' she put in firmly.

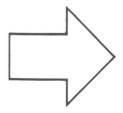

NO COST! NO OBLIGATION TO BUY! NO PURCHASE NECESSARY!

PLAY "LUCKY 7" AND GET FIVE FREE GIFT

HOW TO PLAY:

1. With a coin, carefully scratch off the silver box at the right. Then check the claim chart to see what we have for you—FREE BOOKS and a gift—ALL YOURS! ALL FREE!

2. Send back this card and you'll receive brand-new Harlequin Presents® novels. These books have a cover price of $2.99 each, but they are yours to keep absolutely free.

3. There's no catch. You're under no obligation to buy anything. We charge nothing—ZERO—for your first shipment. And you don't have to make any minimum number of purchases—not even one!

4. The fact is thousands of readers enjoy receiving books by mail from the Harlequin Reader Service®. They like the convenience of home delivery . . . they like getting the best new novels months before they're available in stores . . . and they love our discount prices!

5. We hope that after receiving your free books you'll want to remain a subscriber. But the choice is yours—to continue or cancel, anytime at all! So why not take us up on our invitation, with no risk of any kind. You'll be glad you did!

NOT ACTUAL SIZE

*You'll look like a million dollars
when you wear this lovely necklace!
Its cobra-link chain is a generous
18" long, and the multi-faceted Austrian
crystal sparkles like a diamond!*

**Just scratch off the silver box with a coin.
Then check below to see the gifts you get.**

YES! I have scratched off the silver box. Please send me all the
gifts for which I qualify. I understand I am under no obligation to
purchase any books, as explained on the back and on the opposite
page.

106 CIH AQWL
(U-H-P-10/94)

NAME

ADDRESS   APT.

CITY   STATE   ZIP

7 7 7	**WORTH FOUR FREE BOOKS PLUS A FREE CRYSTAL PENDANT NECKLACE**
🍒🍒🍒	**WORTH THREE FREE BOOKS**
●●●	**WORTH TWO FREE BOOKS**
🔔🔔🍒	**WORTH ONE FREE BOOK**

THE HARLEQUIN READER SERVICE®: HERE'S HOW IT WORKS

Accepting free books places you under no obligation to buy anything. You may keep the books and gift and return the shipping statement marked "cancel". If you do not cancel, about a month later we'll send you 6 additional novels, and bill you just $2.44 each plus 25¢ delivery and applicable sales tax, if any.* That's the complete price, and—compared to cover prices of $2.99 each—quite a bargain! You may cancel at any time, but if you choose to continue, every month we'll send you 6 more books, which you may either purchase at the discount price...or return at our expense and cancel your subscription.

*Terms and prices subject to change without notice. Sales tax applicable in N.Y.

Raff shook his head. 'You became my responsibility the night you stepped off the pavement in front of my car.'

She stood up abruptly, moving across the room to pick up the typewriter from the table where she usually worked. 'I release you from that responsibility,' she told him hardly. 'Now, if you'll give me the sheets of notes you've already completed, I'll get to work on them.' She supported the typewriter on her wrist while holding out her hand for the sheets of paper.

Raff gave them to her. 'Where are you going with that?' He nodded at the typewriter.

'To work on the dining-room table, if that's all right with you,' she replied.

'You won't disturb me if you stay in here,' he assured her.

Maybe not, but he would disturb her! She couldn't be in the same room as him and not be deeply aware of him, would never be able to work with him sitting just behind her.

'I would rather go in the other room,' she said stubbornly, turning to leave.

'Jane.' He stopped her huskily.

She turned slightly.

'Don't do anything foolish,' he warned gruffly, his expression harsh.

He believed she was meeting her ex-lover in town tomorrow!

Well, if he thought she was going to be tempted back to the life she had led in London, he was mistaken. It was strange really, she didn't miss her life there at all. Oh, she missed Jordan, wished there weren't this rift between them, but she didn't miss any other part of the life she had had with him.

She didn't want to even think about how much part her growing attraction for Raff played in that.

If she were about to do anything foolish, it was here with Raff, not in London! Falling in love with him would have to be the most foolish thing she had ever done in her life.

'I won't,' she assured him now.

'And that report is highly confidential,' he reminded her again.

She frowned at his persistence in repeating those words, as if she were going to run out into the street and shout it to all and sundry!

But the reason for Raff's persistence in the need for complete confidentiality became clear to her in the very first paragraph of his report.

Raff was proposing to turn the house into a hotel, the grounds into a sports complex, part of it given over to a golf course!

Jane avidly read through the rest of the report, realising from its content that Raff was putting together a package to present to the banks in the hope of securing the financial backing he would need for such an ambitious idea.

And it did sound very ambitious indeed, although Jane didn't doubt that if anyone could make a success of it Raff could—she was sure he had the ability to make anything he set his mind to succeed. But he had to get considerable financial backing first. And that could be the problem.

And how would the rest of the family feel about having the estate turned into a luxury resort?

'They don't know about it yet.'

Jane looked up sharply at the sound of Raff's softly spoken words, her hair moving silkily against her spine, loose tonight, although the black dress she had on was worn more for comfort than effect, despite the fact that the dark colour made her hair look like flame.

Raff stood framed in the dining-room doorway, although he moved further into the room and closed the door firmly behind him as she looked at him, running a hand through the already tangled thickness of his dark hair. 'I knew as soon as you had read even a part of that report that you would begin to wonder about the rest of the family,' he explained heavily.

Jane moistened her lips. 'It all sounds wonderful.' What else could she say?

He gave a humourless smile. 'But not quite what my dear aunt has in mind, hm?'

She doubted it very much. It would seem slightly vulgar to a woman like Anita Barnes to have the estate turned into a hotel complex, even if it were of a most luxurious standard!

Raff shook his head. 'I'm running out of ideas of how to hold on to this money-gobbling pile.' He looked about him as if, at that moment, he felt he was a prisoner of circumstances.

'Don't your aunt and uncle have money?' Jane suggested tentatively.

His mouth twisted. 'Not enough for the money-monster,' he dismissed. 'No, the estate has to be turned around so that it can begin to support itself. Farming the land doesn't work, and we certainly don't own enough properties to keep things going.' He gave an impatient shrug. 'I don't even know if this idea is viable really, I'm leaving it to the banks to decide that.'

Oh, it all sounded viable, was just the sort of place that had become so popular with her London crowd the last few years, all of the facilities in one place for the 'idle rich' to play with. But if Raff went through with making the estate into a leisure complex it would no longer belong solely to the Quinlan family, and the privacy here would be gone forever.

'Is it what you want?' she probed gently.

'It isn't a question of what I want,' he dismissed irritably. 'My choices are limited.'

Jane chewed on her bottom lip, remembering the conversation about the estate she had had with

Robert at the weekend. 'How do you think the rest of the family will feel about this?'

Raff frowned. 'You mean Anita and Co?'

She repressed a smile at this description; it wasn't really a time for humour. 'That's who I mean,' she nodded.

He sighed. 'I'm not blind to the aspirations Anita has towards the estate, I just don't intend obliging her by popping off before I've had at least my "three score years and ten", and in the meantime the estate has to survive—in any way that it can,' he added grimly. 'The same way I do.'

Jane nodded. 'The leisure complex would be one way of doing that.'

'What do you think of the idea?' He watched her with narrowed eyes.

'Me?' She looked startled. What did she know about such things—more to the point, what did *he* think she knew?

He shrugged. 'I just thought you might have had more experience of places like this than I have.'

Jane's mouth twisted. 'With my designer-label clothes, silk underwear, and rich lovers, you mean?' she said drily.

Raff looked irritated. 'Perhaps I was a little hasty in those assumptions,' he muttered.

Amusement darkened her eyes at this be-grudging almost-apology. 'Were you?'

'To tell you the truth——' he crossed the room to her abruptly '—I'm getting to the stage where I don't really care any more!'

Jane looked up at him with wide eyes, knowing he was going to kiss her again. And each time he did her defences got a little weaker. She was falling in love with this man. And it seemed as inevitable as that very first night they had met. Almost a fated attraction. The chances of their meeting any other way had to be extremely remote.

His hands were gentle as he raised her face for his kiss, their mouths moving together in gentle exploration until hunger took over, her hands entwined in the dark thickness of his hair as she held him close to her.

Raff's eyes glowed darkly as he looked down at her. 'A few centuries ago you would have been burnt as a witch,' he murmured gruffly, his face relaxed in languid passion.

The only time he seemed to relax at all!

'Why?' Jane prompted. But she knew, she knew... But she just needed to hear from his lips that he was as affected by their kisses as she was.

His mouth tightened, as if he regretted kissing her at all, and he moved away from her abruptly. 'Will you have dinner with me tomorrow night?' he asked abruptly.

There was no reason why she shouldn't have returned from town by then, but it was the unexpectedness of the invitation that made her hesitate.

'Why?' she said again.

'Oh, for God's sake, Jane!' He strode away impatiently. 'Does there have to be a reason?'

She looked at him consideringly, knowing he didn't like having his motives questioned like this. But she was so uncertain...

'I think so, yes,' she nodded.

He scowled. 'Why don't you just accept before I come to my senses?'

That was partly what she was afraid of. It also seemed too much of a coincidence to her that he should want to take her out tomorrow evening, when he more than suspected she was meeting a man during her trip into London. The last thing she was going to feel like after a lunch with Jordan was answering yet more questions, about him this time!

'Ask me again after tomorrow,' she told Raff wearily.

He frowned, thrusting his hands into his trouser-pockets. 'What will your answer be?'

'Yes. Probably.' She grimaced.

'Then answer me now,' he instructed abruptly. 'Either you do want to come out to dinner with me or you don't. I'm not about to repeat the invitation.'

Ever, he left unsaid. But the implication was there all the same.

'Yes,' she said abruptly, hating this feeling of manipulation, knowing that if she didn't feel so attracted to him that he would never get away with it. As she dared not let him think that he had this time either! 'But not tomorrow,' she added firmly. 'Wednesday, instead.' She named the day after tomorrow, her head held high in challenge as anger darkened his features.

'Why is that?' he derided. 'Expecting to be too tired to go out to dinner when you get back tomorrow?'

His insult was clear, and it took all Jane's effort of will not to tell him exactly what he could do with his dinner invitation, knowing that if she did there might never be another one. And she was too attracted to him to want to do that...

She met his gaze unflinchingly. 'I expect to be less than good company after the drive and a little shopping in town, yes,' she nodded.

His eyes blazed, and Jane knew he wanted to rant and rave at her about the stupidity of meeting Jordan at all. But he didn't, although anger emanated from every pore of his body. 'Wednesday night,' he bit out coldly. 'Eight o'clock,' he added sharply before slamming out of the room.

Jane sat back weakly, feeling emotionally drained.

She had just never met a man quite like Raff before. And that was the problem.

The man who most closely resembled Raff sat across the restaurant table from her, had already been seated at their usual table when she arrived

ten minutes late for their one o'clock luncheon
appointment.

She knew Jordan would have arrived precisely
on time, been shown to the table by Henry, who
knew them both so well, and she also knew that
Jordan had made a great pretence of looking at the
menu, all the time his anger burning coldly under
the surface as the minutes ticked away, signalling
her tardiness.

For Jordan had known she would come, that although she might be late she would definitely meet
him here.

Jordan had changed little in the two weeks since
she'd last seen him. And he should have looked different, his hair should have grown longer—something, anything to show that time had elapsed for
him too. But Jordan always looked the same, always
neat, always impeccable, never a hair out of place,
that rich dark hair always kept the same short
length, although Jane had never been able to work
out when he fitted these visits to the hairdresser
into his busy working schedule. He probably paid
someone to visit his office and cut his hair while
he continued to work!

After Raff's unkempt look, his hair over-long and
certainly not kept in any particular style, Jordan
looked even more austerely impeccable than ever!

But she loved him anyway. Had always loved
him.

She still wasn't sure how she felt towards Raff.

'Well?' Jordan barked, his patience—what there was of it!—finally at an end.

Jane smiled at him brightly; she had never been cowed by him the way other people seemed to be. And he knew it. 'I was glad you telephoned,' she told him lightly. 'I have something I want to talk to you about.'

'*You* have——'

'Jordan, please.' She mockingly interrupted his explosion. 'People are staring,' she taunted.

'I don't give a damn what other people are doing,' he grated fiercely, although it was noticeable that he had lowered his voice slightly, grey-blue eyes glittering angrily at being goaded into losing the strict control he usually kept over his temper. 'I want to know what you think you're playing at?'

Her eyes widened innocently, on her own territory now, supremely confident among the other rich patrons of this exclusive restaurant, dressed in the 'designer label' clothes Raff had so scorned.

Strangely enough she had a feeling Raff and Jordan would actually get on well together, despite their differences in lifestyle and the seven or eight years' difference in their ages. They were very alike in so many other ways; maybe that was one of the reasons she found Raff so rakishly attractive.

She sobered at the thought. 'I'm not playing at all, Jordan,' she said softly. 'I have a feeling my game-playing days are over,' she added ruefully.

His eyes narrowed suspiciously. 'What do you mean by that?'

She shrugged off the importance of her statement—maybe because she didn't want to admit what the answer really was.

She drew in a deep breath. 'What can you tell me about the chances of success at turning a substantial manor house and its grounds into a going concern as a hotel and leisure complex?'

Jordan's mouth twisted sardonically. 'A little premature, aren't you?'

'Hm?' She gave him a vague frown, still deep in thought, barely noticing as the drinks he had ordered arrived at the table, the menu still closed in front of her.

'Spending your inheritance already?' he mocked. 'There's still ten weeks to go to your birthday.'

Jane gave him an impatient look. 'I'm not asking for myself.'

His frown turned to one of puzzlement. 'Then who?'

She sighed at his persistence. 'A—friend.' Telling Jordan to mind his own business would just result in her not getting any answers from him at all, and if anyone could advise her as to the viability of Raff's proposal it would be Jordan.

'Who owns a country residence he wouldn't mind converting?' Jordan mused shrewdly.

'I don't believe I said it was a he,' she bristled defensively.

Jordan gave her a scornful look. 'Would you bother to ask at all if it were a she?'

Now it was Jane's turn to frown. 'I'm not sure I like your implication.'

'No?'

His cool mockery annoyed her immensely; she hadn't been as selfish in the past as he was implying...had she? If she had, meeting Raff had changed all that!

'Jordan, just answer my original question,' she said irritably.

'This job you have,' he spoke thoughtfully. 'It's at the Quinlan house, a large manor house with thousands of acres of land attached. This "friend" you're talking about wouldn't be Rafferty Quinlan, would it?' Jordan's eyes were narrowed.

Jane gave a start of surprise—couldn't help herself—although she didn't know why she should feel in the least surprised that Jordan should know about the house and Raff; she should have realised that in the two days since Jordan had found out her whereabouts he would have found out everything he could about the house and its occupants. Nevertheless, she felt slightly disconcerted, and she certainly didn't want to get into a lengthy discussion about Raff.

'Do you have to know everything?' she attacked.

'Yes!' Jordan bit out forcefully.

Jane sighed. 'Why can't you just answer a straightforward business question?'

'Maybe because "business questions" are the last thing I expect from you,' he snapped. 'You've never shown the slightest interest before.'

She grimaced at the truth of that. And maybe it wasn't a good enough excuse that *he* had never shown the slightest inclination to discuss business with *her*. It was just possible, she could see in retrospect, that Jordan might not have spent so many nights closeted alone in his study if she had been willing to listen and talk to him about any problems he may have had. Raff had certainly done so when she had given him the opportunity, and how much closer her relationship with Jordan than it had ever been with Raff!

'I'm sorry for that.' She put her hand over his much stronger one as it rested on the table-top, his fingers long and tapered. 'But won't you help me now?'

He looked at her searchingly, as if this were the last thing he had expected of her. And maybe it was. Jane began to wonder just how selfish she had been over the years. And to wonder at the reason for the change in her...

Jordan drew in a deep breath. 'If it is the Quinlan house you're talking about—let's just theoretically say that it is...' he added drily at her stubbornly defensive expression.

Despite all the odds, Raff had trusted her with a confidence, and she couldn't go breaking that now.

The only trouble with that was that to be able to help Raff in the way she would like to she had to at least discuss this with Jordan, his knowledge of these things being so much more superior than either Raff's or her own.

'... The size of the building, the considerable grounds,' Jordan continued firmly. 'The right location—not too far from London, basically—I think it would stand a very good chance of success as a leisure centre, with the right backing. I think it could succeed very well,' he nodded thoughtfully.

Jane was satisfied with that answer, confident in Jordan's opinion; anything he touched seemed to turn to gold, and if he thought the venture could succeed then it would.

'As you don't appear to be going to enlighten me any further on that subject,' Jordan continued harshly, 'perhaps we had better get back to the original one.'

Jane removed her hand from his. 'Which was?' she prompted wearily, only too familiar with his stubborn determination.

He impatiently waved the waiter away from taking their order, which was probably the third time he had done so in the last fifteen minutes or so; the way things were going they wouldn't get to actually eat at all!

'What did you think you were doing,' Jordan attacked as soon as the waiter had gone, his voice so controlled it was dangerous, 'just taking off like that?'

She turned from giving the poor, downcast waiter a sympathetic smile, the smile fading. '*You* told me I had to get a job and prove myself capable of doing so before I was twenty-one,' she reminded him accusingly, 'or you would have no choice but to advise the trustees of Father's will to hold my money over until I'm twenty-five!'

'You weren't supposed to just take off like that after I'd issued the challenge,' he rasped.

'Wasn't I?' she shrugged. 'I thought I was.'

'You could have let me know where you were. *How* you were,' Jordan snapped.

'But I did,' she reasoned.

'A week after you'd disappeared!' he said impatiently. 'Good God, you could have been kidnapped for all I knew of your whereabouts.'

Jane smiled as she remembered she had thought that might be a possibility herself that night she had met Raff and he had just taken her off so arrogantly—and how she had doubted Jordan would pay any ransom demand.

'It isn't funny, damn it!' Jordan misunderstood the reason for her humour, his expression full of anger. 'Not when you consider who you are.'

Who was she? The last few weeks she hadn't really been sure from one minute to the next!

Oh, yes, Rhea-Jane Somerville-Smythe.

As if it weren't ridiculous enough that she had been blighted with one double-barrelled name, her father had chosen to burden her with two!

'You're heiress to a considerable fortune,' Jordan reminded tautly.

Oh, yes, she was that, too.

If she could prove before she was twenty-one that she was capable of being responsible for all that money.

'And you're my sister,' Jordan added forcibly.

Oh, yes, she was that, too...

CHAPTER SEVEN

'As YOU realise, I'm not using my full name,' Rhea-Jane told her brother drily.

'"Jane Smith"!' Jordan said disgustedly.

She glared at him. 'You should try getting a job, any job, with a name like Rhea-Jane Somerville-Smythe. It isn't just difficult, it's impossible! If Father's will hadn't——'

'I've told you already, I'm not responsible for Father's will, only in seeing that his wishes are carried out,' Jordan dismissed. 'He would be very upset if he knew that clause in his will had resulted in what it has.'

Rhea-Jane shrugged. 'He didn't leave me much choice. But then, he never did, did he?' Her tone edged on bitterness, although it was an emotion she had always shied away from where her father was concerned; he just hadn't liked her, and there had been nothing she could do about it.

Her brother sighed. 'You were a rebellious little madam.'

'And he never forgave me for Mother dying when I was born,' she defended heatedly.

Jordan's hard face softened slightly. 'He was never any different, Rhea.' He used that first part of her name affectionately, as most people did who knew her well. 'I had to prove myself time and time again as being worthy to carry on after him.'

And it hadn't embittered him. Or had it? Jordan was even more difficult to know than Raff was, and he had no confidants, talked to Rhea if he talked things over with anyone. She had never thought about it before, but perhaps that too was as a result of having the father they'd had.

Jordan looked at her sympathetically. 'But I suppose I did have the advantage of having a mother who loved me unquestioningly for the first eight years of my life,' he realised gently.

Rhea-Jane gave a regretful smile. 'I wish I had known her.' She frowned as she recalled several conversations she had had lately that had disturbed her, conversations that she had so far been unable to confirm as being about her mother. 'She was a nanny before she married Father, wasn't she?' she probed as lightly as she was able.

'Rhea.' Jordan looked at her warningly. 'You're just trying to divert attention from yourself; we haven't talked about Mother and Father for years.'

'But I never knew Mummy——'

'Rhea, it's almost twenty-one years since she died,' Jordan cut in impatiently. 'I barely remember her myself!'

'But do you know if she ever happened to work for the Quinlan family?' Rhea-Jane persisted exasperatedly.

'The Quinlans?' he frowned. 'Why on earth should she have worked for them?'

She shrugged irritably. 'It's just that I seem to remind several members of the family of someone they used to know, and someone came up with the name of Raff's old nanny. It was Diana.' Her eyes darkened.

She had just enough doubt in her mind that it could actually have been her mother for her to need to find out positively; it was going to look very odd to Raff if her mother should turn out to be the woman who had once been involved with his father! He wasn't likely to believe that she hadn't known of the relationship, judging by the way he already distrusted women so badly.

'That's ridiculous,' Jordan dismissed scornfully. 'Why on earth should that Diana have been Mother?'

Why indeed? And yet she had this nagging doubt at the back of her mind that wouldn't let her rest easy about the subject. But she didn't think Jordan would welcome any suggestion from her that their mother might once have had a relationship with Donald Quinlan, especially as the other man had been married at the time; Jordan had absolutely idolised their mother.

'I don't suppose it's really important,' Rhea-Jane told her brother lightly. 'I only mentioned it in passing. The important thing is that you think this leisure-complex project could succeed...'

'I said it stands a very good chance,' Jordan corrected firmly. 'With the right backing. I would need to know a lot more about it before I gave my considered opinion.'

'I'm typing up a report on it for Raff right now—— What's so funny?' she demanded as she saw Jordan begin to smile.

His mouth quirked. 'So that expensive finishing-school is starting to pay off at last,' he derided. 'What's your typing speed?'

'Very funny, Jordan,' she snapped. 'Don't worry, I'll never be any threat to Glenda.' She mentioned his secretary's name.

'I would never employ you, anyway,' he told her bluntly. 'I don't believe in nepotism. But I would be very interested in seeing a copy of that report.' He looked at her steadily.

She sighed her indecision. 'It's a very confidential report...'

'You've told me most of the details already,' he reminded her. 'So you may as well let me have a look at the rest of them,' he encouraged.

'Well...' She hesitated.

'I give you my word it will go no further.'

When Jordan put it like that...! She knew that when he gave his word he meant it.

She nodded. 'I'm going to finish typing it when I get back this afternoon; I'll try and get a copy off to you before the last post.'

He looked at her consideringly. 'You seem very concerned that this Raff Quinlan should succeed?'

'Just give me your opinion on the report, and stop trying to make something out of nothing,' said Jane, her cheeks flushed.

'Is it nothing?' Jordan probed.

Her head went back defensively. 'Yes!'

But she knew that it wasn't, knew without doubt that she was teetering on the edge of falling in love with Raff.

'Where exactly did you go yesterday?' Raff rasped, his eyes narrowed to steely slits. 'Or did you just get bored with the present company, and feel a need to see your rich boyfriend again?'

He had been dying to throw that accusation at her since she had first asked for the day off! Of course, she could just tell him that Jordan was her older brother, but if she did that she would have to tell him everything, and if she did *that* he was sure to ask her to leave, clause in her father's will or not!

And how could she help Raff if she was forced to leave? Because she was sure, once Jordan had read the report she had sent off to him the previous evening, that she would be able to offer Raff firm advice about the conversion of the estate into a leisure complex, albeit if that information had come from Jordan.

But Raff wasn't likely to let Rhea-Jane Somerville-Smythe stay on here and offer him that help.

Her family was well-known in the City, Jordan even more successful than their father had been, their business acumen notorious, their wealth even more so. The Somerville-Smythes were an 'old' family, part of the 'establishment', and Jordan was a worthy successor as head of that family, was highly respected, and would be furiously angry to learn he had been called any woman's 'rich boyfriend' in that condescending way! If there were any women in Jordan's life he was extremely discreet about them.

Rhea-Jane had known Raff's mood was suspect when she'd met him earlier to go out, but he had said nothing on the drive to this country restaurant, nor while they'd perused the menu and ordered their meal. What conversation he had made had been polite in the extreme. She should have become wary as soon as she'd realised that!

Instead, as they'd waited for their food to be served, Raff's question had come straight for the jugular.

She was still reeling slightly from her meeting with Jordan, her brother wanting to know every detail of her job before he would let her go, his 'Goodbye, Jane Smith' a timely reminder as she left that he would be keeping a close eye on her in future, that he wasn't about to put an end to what she was trying to do just yet, but that he reserved the right to do so if he deemed it necessary.

'I wasn't bored at all,' she answered Raff's question calmly enough.

His expression was stony. 'Mrs Howard tells me that you had a telephone call before you felt this sudden need to go into London.'

She shouldn't really be surprised that the housekeeper had told Raff about the call, knowing that the other woman had probably felt honour-bound to do so; Jane was, after all, an employee in Raff's house, and they knew so little about her that the telephone call had probably seemed important to the other woman. Nevertheless, things would have been much easier if Raff had never known of the telephone call.

But, then, when had life ever been made easier for her?

'I did receive a telephone call, yes——'

'From the man you ran away from in the first place?' Raff cut in harshly.

She blushed. 'I didn't run away from him——'

'All right, the man you left so abruptly that you had to stay in a hotel because you had nowhere else to go!' he altered impatiently. 'It all adds up to the same thing; you had left the man, but as soon as you received a telephone call from him you rushed off to London to see him.'

'I had a good reason for meeting him,' she defended, deciding it was pointless to waste time arguing with him over what Jordan had, or had not, been in her life.

His mouth twisted with distaste. 'I'm sure you did.'

Rhea-Jane gave a rueful smile. 'Careful, Raff,' she murmured. 'Your prejudice is starting to show.'

He took a large swallow of the whisky and water that had just been delivered to him, not even wincing as the fiery liquid passed down his throat.

Rhea-Jane sipped at her own glass of white wine, looking at Raff over its rim. 'Actually,' she added softly, 'I wanted to talk to him about you.' She deliberately avoided using any names, sure that Raff was just as capable of making enquiries as Jordan was—and, if he did, that he would discover who she was and throw her out.

'Me?' Raff looked at her suspiciously. 'You talked about me?'

'I didn't mention your name,' she told him truthfully; after all, Jordan had been the one to actually introduce Raff's name to the conversation.

'Why the hell did I come into your conversation at all?' Raff burst out impatiently. 'I don't think I care to be discussed by you and your friends!'

He made the latter sound like an actual insult!

'You weren't discussed at all,' she bristled. 'I believe I said you were mentioned.' She made this sound deliberately insulting, too.

Raff's mouth tightened ominously. 'But in what context?'

'In the context of my employer,' she snapped, goaded into being defensive, giving up any idea of discussing Jordan's opinion with Raff this evening. 'What other context is there?' she scorned.

'Just what, exactly,' he spoke in a level tone—too level, 'did you *mention* about me?'

He was likely to explode with temper if he thought she had discussed his personal business with anyone, even if it had been with good intentions. And from the look of him it wouldn't do any good to assure him Jordan could be discretion itself when he chose to be; she could tell from Raff's mood that he wouldn't believe she had acted out of a desire to help him.

'I told you——' her gaze was evasive, but she couldn't help it, hating having to lie '—I told him you were my employer.'

'For what purpose?' Raff grated.

'For *no* purpose,' she said exasperatedly.

His eyes were narrowed. 'Then why talk about me at all?'

Jane gave a weary sigh. 'I think perhaps it would be better if we just forgot about dinner and left now.'

He looked at her intently, grudging respect slowly entering his eyes as he did so. 'You mean it, don't you?' he said in some surprise.

'Of course I mean it,' she snapped impatiently. 'I didn't exactly enjoy my lunch out yesterday.' They had finally got around to eating, but by that time

Rhea-Jane didn't feel like it, merely picking at the salad she had ordered. She didn't think she was going to fare any better this evening after the conversation they had just had!

'But I would like to enjoy my dinner, and it looks as if I have to go back to the house to do that!' she finished.

The grudging respect turned to amusement as Raff began to smile. 'Wouldn't you rather enjoy the steak you have just ordered here?'

'Yes, I would rather,' she mimicked mockingly. 'If I'm allowed to?'

Raff held up his hands defensively. 'I'm hungry too, so how about a truce?'

She couldn't be bothered at this moment to point out to him that to call a truce they both had to have been at war—and *she* certainly hadn't been intending to fight with anyone this evening. Intentions, and what actually happened, when this man was about, were two entirely different things, as she had already learned too well.

She gave a weary shrug. 'A truce it is—as long as I can eat my dinner in peace!' Her eyes flashed warningly.

He relaxed visibly. 'Dinner in peace it is,' he conceded teasingly.

Actually, she had been let off the hook easier than she had hoped after his anger of a few minutes ago; she had expected Raff to pursue the subject of her luncheon with this unnamed friend of hers until he had the answers he sought.

The least Raff and Jordan knew about each other the better!

Strange really, because she was sure, despite their differences, that the two men would at least respect each other.

But she very much doubted they would ever get to meet each other, for ten weeks from now she would just be an unpleasant memory for Raff!

As it was, they had an enjoyable evening after all; a lovely meal, pleasant conversation, both of them seeming to want to steer clear of any subject that might prove volatile. Which seriously limited the things they could talk about, but at least there were no more arguments!

'What do I tell Mrs Howard about our dinner out this evening?' Rhea-Jane asked on the drive back to the house, having left it to Raff earlier to tell the other woman they wouldn't be at home for the meal. But she didn't think she would escape so easily tomorrow morning when she had coffee in the kitchen with the other woman as usual.

Raff glanced at her as he sat behind the wheel of the car. 'Maybe we should just tell her that I invited you out tonight because I just couldn't keep my hands off you any longer.'

Rhea-Jane's mouth quirked at his mockery. 'That's hardly true.'

'The evening isn't over yet!' He raised those dark brows suggestively.

She laughed softly at his teasing, the laughter dying in her throat as he didn't return the humour, but simply met her gaze steadily for several seconds before returning his attention to the road.

The car was suddenly charged with tension, a sexual awareness that made Rhea-Jane shiver with anticipation.

Except for a single light left on outside the front door, and another in the hallway, the house seemed to be in darkness when they got in, Mrs Howard obviously having retired for the evening.

Raff refused Rhea-Jane's offer to make them both coffee.

She didn't know what she was supposed to do now. Should she just go to bed? She wasn't sure.

'Let's go into the lounge for a few minutes,' said Raff, instantly solving her indecision for her, entering the darkened room ahead of her to switch on the two side-lamps that gave off a warm glow.

Rhea-Jane eyed him a little apprehensively, not altogether sure she should be alone with him like this. If he should kiss her again . . .! But apart from that remark in the car just now he had given no indication during the rest of the evening that he wanted to do any such thing, she chided herself.

'I enjoyed tonight.' He broke the silence.

'Don't sound so surprised,' she scolded mockingly. Really, to listen to him it sounded as if there was something wrong with enjoying her company! They had had a bumpy start to the evening, but it had certainly progressed smoothly after that.

He sat down next to her on the sofa. 'Do you have any idea how long it is since I actually enjoyed a woman's company?'

She would hazard a guess at it being some time ago, judging from his instant distrust of women, and yet he must have had *some* happy moments with his wife.

'In any capacity,' he added gruffly.

Rhea-Jane swallowed hard, not sure she wanted to hear this. The thought of him with another woman—in any capacity!—suddenly made her feel ill. Oh, she knew he wouldn't have been celibate before his marriage, or after, and yet she felt an overwhelming resentment towards any other women who had been in his life.

It was quite frightening to realise how jealous she felt.

'Why do I find *you* attractive?' Raff entwined his fingers in her hair, staring at it as if fascinated. 'I wish I knew more about you,' he frowned darkly.

'The little you do know, you dislike,' she reminded him lightly. She had avoided being trapped into revealing who she was once tonight, she wasn't going to fail now.

'I've never said that,' he rasped, his fingers tightening.

'Lust can be a great incentive to memory lapses,' Rhea-Jane scorned hardly.

His mouth firmed. 'I wish it were only lust I were talking about.'

She frowned at him, her gaze searching his face. 'What do you mean?'

He shook his head, pulling her slowly towards him.

This was what he meant, this instantaneous attraction that neither of them seemed able to control!

Rhea-Jane trembled in his arms, her senses reeling as the warmth of his lips claimed hers.

Every time she was with him like this it was as if she had come home after a long journey.

Raff groaned low in his throat, deepening the kiss, caressing her back with restless hands.

It was Rhea-Jane's turn to groan as one of those hands moved to cup her breast, desire coursing through her body, her limbs filled with a melting warmth that quickly spread through her whole body.

The pad of his thumb moved rhythmically across the tip of her breast, causing her to gasp as the hardening of her body betrayed her—if her response hadn't already done that!

'Raff...!' She drew in a sharp breath.

'I know, I know,' he muttered, laying her gently back on the sofa, his lips moving down her throat to the sensitive hollows below, his tongue caressing the smooth skin there erotically.

His hair was silky-soft beneath her fingers, her body arching against him as his lips closed over the hardened tip of her breast through her dress, the sensation of that rasping tongue through the silk material unlike any pleasure she had ever known before.

Raff half lay across her, his body hard with desire, a desire that shook his body as she moved against him, entwining her legs with his, letting her shoes drop to the floor, curving herself against him, wanting to be closer still.

Raff looked down at her with dark eyes. 'I can't make love to you here.'

She blinked up at him, the spell broken. She was stupid, or naïve; it hadn't occurred to her that Raff would want to make love to her.

'Mrs Howard might walk in.' He misconstrued her silence as disappointment, attempting to explain his reluctance in case she should misunderstand him.

Raff wanted to make love to her.

What would he say when he discovered the assumptions he had made about her morals were completely wrong?

It wasn't that she was a prude, or even that she had never been tempted. A couple of years ago she had been very tempted, but the man in question had decided she was too young at eighteen to know what she was doing. He had been forty-two, and already married; in fact, his own daughter had been one of her friends, her contemporary, so the infatuation had died a death several weeks later.

Almost three years later she was still a virgin.

Because there hadn't been a single man in all that time she wanted to make that sort of commitment to.

Was Raff that man?

Oh, yes . . .

'Jane?'

She looked at him dazedly. She *loved* this man, loved Raff Quinlan.

'Jane, I——' He broke off as a knock sounded on the door, getting quickly to his feet and standing slightly in front of Rhea-Jane so that she could compose herself as Mrs Howard came into the room.

'Yes?' he prompted tersely, and Jane felt sorry for the other woman; she couldn't possibly have known what she was interrupting—again!

And it was just as well they had been interrupted; she might have ended up babbling her love for this man otherwise!

Poor Mrs Howard looked flustered. 'I heard you come in, and I thought you might like some coffee . . .' she trailed off awkwardly.

Rhea-Jane stood up, smiling reassuringly at the other woman. 'That sounds like a lovely idea,' she encouraged.

The housekeeper turned to leave thankfully, hesitating only slightly before turning back to Raff.

'There were a couple of telephone calls for you while you were out, I left the numbers for you to return the calls on your desk.' She frowned. 'One man seemed rather insistent, although he wouldn't leave his name.'

Raff looked as if business calls were the last thing he wanted to deal with right now!

But Rhea-Jane needed a little time to collect her thoughts together! 'I'll come and help you with the coffee while Raff makes his call,' she told the housekeeper, deliberately avoiding Raff's gaze as she followed the other woman out of the room.

'There's really no need,' Mrs Howard protested.

There was every need, if she were to end this evening with any degree of decorum. Besides, she felt she owed the other woman some sort of explanation. After all, she had been so insistent that she was only an employee, like Mrs Howard herself, this last week, and tonight she had calmly been out to dinner with her 'boss'!

'I would like to help,' she smiled, walking ahead to the kitchen.

Mrs Howard still seemed flustered as she moved about the room preparing the tray while Rhea-Jane filled the percolator. 'I really didn't mean to intrude just now,' the housekeeper burst out, obviously uncomfortable with the whole situation.

'You didn't.' Rhea-Jane touched her arm, giving it a little reassuring squeeze. 'Raff and I were just discussing business.' Surely she could be forgiven that lie, for the sake of this woman's embarrassment?

'I don't know,' she began uncertainly. 'Raff didn't seem at all pleased, and—— Raff?' Her shocked gaze focused over Rhea-Jane's left shoulder. 'What on earth has happened?' she gasped.

Rhea-Jane understood the other woman's concern as soon as she herself turned to look at Raff, his expression like thunder. And it was, she realised, directed straight at her!

'I want to talk to you, Jane. Alone,' he grated forcefully. 'Now!'

'Really, Raff——'

'It's all right, Mrs Howard,' Rhea-Jane softly re-assured her as she left the kitchen, her gaze never leaving Raff's pale, angry face.

Although she felt far from reassured herself as she followed Raff to his study, his back rigid with fury. What had she done now? How could he have changed so much in just a few short minutes?

He sat down abruptly on the front of his desk as she closed the door behind her, just looking at her for several long, tension-filled moments. Rhea-Jane could feel the moisture making her spine sticky, sensing the violence within him that was barely held in check.

What had *happened*? Had he, somehow, realised who she was, and wanted an explanation?

She drew in a ragged breath. 'Raff——'

'The "rich friend" you met yesterday...' his voice was dangerously soft when he at last spoke '... It wouldn't have been Jordan Somerville-Smythe, would it?' His eyes narrowed.

She paled. How could he possibly——?

'I can see by your face that it was,' Raff bit out contemptuously, his mouth twisted with disgust. '"In the context of being my employer",' he mimicked grotesquely. '"What other context is there?"' he continued challengingly. 'The context of my private business, that I had *entrusted* you with!' he accused heatedly, sitting forward now, his hands clenched into fists at his sides.

He *knew* she had discussed the possibility of the estate's being turned into a leisure complex with Jordan! But how——?

Jordan himself, she realised with a sick feeling in the pit of her stomach. *He* had been the man who'd telephoned Raff earlier this evening and hadn't given a name.

But he had given one now!

He had read the report she'd sent him, and not wasted any time after that in trying to talk to her, but had contacted Raff directly.

Oh, Jordan...

CHAPTER EIGHT

JANE moistened dry lips, realising she was in serious trouble this time, feeling hot and cold at the same time. 'Raff——'

'I *trusted* you, damn it!' His fist landed heavily on the desk at his side. 'I trusted you, and you took the first opportunity you could to run off and tell your rich boyfriend every damn detail!'

'I——'

'Don't even attempt to deny it,' he warned coldly. 'I know it had to be you who talked to him because the report I sent the bank hasn't had time to reach them yet!'

She realised that, and the only thing to Jordan's credit in all this seemed to be that he hadn't betrayed the very vital confidence of just exactly who she was and what she was to him.

But it wasn't much of a credit, because it no longer seemed so very important; Raff was going to want her to leave after this, anyway.

'He actually telephoned here,' Raff continued incredulously. 'Had the audacity to offer me a business deal!'

That sounded like the Jordan she knew and loved! Although she could cheerfully have strangled him at that moment. But he wouldn't really have thought about the damage he could be doing, she knew that; Jordan functioned on a business level only most of the time. And he obviously thought the leisure complex a good business venture.

She looked at Raff curiously. 'What was your reply?'

'What was——? Jane, you broke a confidence!' Raff stood up furiously.

Rhea-Jane held her ground. 'I did it with good intentions. Jordan is an excellent business-man——'

'I'm well aware of who he is,' Raff cut in coldly.

Exactly who he was? Did he know Jordan was Diana's son?

She shrugged. 'Then you must realise how competent he is. I actually only asked him about the viability of a leisure complex, I had no idea he would be interested in investing in it himself.'

Although possibly she should have done; Jordan was first and foremost a businessman. 'What *did* you tell him?' She frowned.

Grey eyes glittered glacially. 'He's coming here tomorrow so that we can discuss it,' Raff revealed defensively, as if he wished he could tell her he had told Jordan to go to hell. But, thankfully, good sense had prevented him from doing that.

Only one thing mattered to Rhea-Jane at that moment; Jordan was coming *here*. Not as her

brother, but as a prospective business partner for
Raff, by the sound of it.

'Is he the one, Jane?' Raff asked tautly.

She looked at him dazedly; the one what?

'The one you were running away from that
night?' he explained harshly.

Colour heated her cheeks. 'I wasn't running away
from him,' she asserted. Although she was aware
it wasn't so far from the truth. She had been trying
to escape the life she had made for herself with
Jordan; she just hadn't realised it at the time.

Raff clearly saw the indecision in her expression.
'Running *to*, then,' he almost accused.

Her eyes flashed at the insult intended. 'I wasn't
running *to* him either!'

'But you did live with him?'

She sighed at his persistence. 'Yes. But not
in——'

'He doesn't know about us?' Raff's eyes were
narrowed, his hands thrust into his denims pockets.

'Us . . .?' she echoed dazedly. 'Raff——'

'I don't think Somerville-Smythe is a man ruled
by his emotions,' he cut in coolly, 'so I'm expecting
our meeting tomorrow to be purely of a business
nature. I would prefer it if anything the two of you
have to say to each other you do in your own time,
and not in mine!'

Rhea-Jane looked at him searchingly. Did that
mean he didn't want her to leave immediately, as
she had expected he would?

He was right about Jordan, though; he certainly wasn't ruled by his heart, and if he thought the leisure complex was a good investment then it almost certainly was. She couldn't have been happier for Raff. Although it certainly hadn't helped her own situation with him. But, knowing her brother as she did, she didn't even think he would see any of this as a problem; he always saw his personal and business life as completely separate things, and functioned accordingly.

She moistened her lips. 'What time are you expecting Jordan to arrive?'

'Mid-morning,' Raff supplied tersely.

She would make sure she was nowhere in sight at that time, had no wish to make the situation any more taut than it obviously already was.

And any relationship she might have thought was delicately forming between herself and Raff was definitely at an end. She didn't need Raff to tell her that, she could see exactly how he felt about her now in his face.

Jordan couldn't have known just how untimely his intrusion had been, but if he thought he was going to get away with doing what he had without being told exactly what Rhea-Jane thought of him, no matter how innocent his motives, he was mistaken!

'What kept you?' he drily received her call a few minutes after she had awkwardly excused herself from Raff, leaving him staring after her broodingly in his study.

Rhea-Jane counted to ten before answering her brother—although it didn't actually seem to cool her anger very much! 'What do you think "kept me"?' she finally challenged.

'I have no idea—Quinlan?' he realised slowly.

'Don't sound so surprised, Jordan,' she scorned. 'How did you expect him to react to me after you had just told him you knew all the details of a report he believed to be completely confidential, and calmly offered him a business deal?'

'In a businesslike manner,' her brother instantly dismissed—as she should have guessed he would!

She wished she could convince Jordan of just how insensitive he had been, but she knew she would be wasting her time and her breath even trying; he just wouldn't understand.

Perhaps it was enough that he realised she was very angry about what he had done.

'You've made my position here very awkward.' She stubbornly hung on to her outrage.

'I don't see——'

'Jordan, I'm your sister!' Her impatient outburst started out high-pitched, and lowered drastically on the last word as Rhea-Jane looked about the hallway guiltily in case anyone should have overheard her. Which was ridiculous. Raff had stormed past her a few minutes ago on the way upstairs to his bedroom, and Mrs Howard would have retired for the night long ago, knowing better than to expect any explanation from Raff for his earlier behaviour.

'I'm well aware of who you are, Rhea,' Jordan began in a bored voice.

'But Raff isn't!' she reminded frustratedly.

'It's time that particular deception came to an end anyway,' Jordan dismissed. 'You've proved your point, Rhea, and I'm more than happy to advise the other trustees of Father's will to release the money to you on your twenty-first birthday.'

She should feel triumphant. Over the moon. It was what she had wanted, what she had entered into this charade for. Her independence. The means to make a life for herself.

But she would have to leave Quinlan House. Leave Raff...

'What if I'm not ready for the "deception" to come to an end?' She tried to make light of it, but knew she had failed miserably!

'Don't be ridiculous, Rhea.' All complacency had left Jordan's voice now, so that he sounded almost as arrogant as Raff himself! 'I can hardly have my sister working as a secretary to my new business partner!'

No, that wouldn't do at all, as far as the Somerville-Smythe pride was concerned, Rhea-Jane acknowledged wryly.

'Has it even occurred to you that he may not want to be your business partner?' she pointed out drily.

'He will,' Jordan returned confidently. 'If he has any business sense at all!'

No arrogance from Jordan this time, just an assurance of his own capabilities. But he hadn't met Raff yet, couldn't quite know what he would be up against, had already antagonised Raff by telephoning in the first place. It was sure to be a case of 'the irresistible force meeting the immovable object' when these two men met!

It might be fun, at that.

It was certainly inevitable.

And if it couldn't be avoided there was no point in trying to run away from it. She certainly wasn't going to make herself scarce tomorrow now, as Raff wanted her to do.

'Although I can't be sure that he does,' Jordan added mockingly. 'After all, he did employ *you* as his secretary!'

'Very funny,' she replied sarcastically. 'We'll see tomorrow, shall we?' she taunted.

'You may as well have your things packed so that you're ready to leave with me after I've spoken to Quinlan,' Jordan advised uninterestedly before ringing off.

Rhea-Jane frowned at the receiver frustratedly as the disengaged tone came on the line.

Jordan had spoken, so it had to be so!

No wonder she had come close to strangling him several times in her life!

But even so, he was probably right about the packing. And she certainly didn't think she was going to sleep, anyway...

She felt as if she were walking on hot coals all morning, unable to even think about concentrating on work, aware of Mrs Howard giving several curious looks in her direction, as she didn't eat anything for breakfast, but poured herself several cups of coffee instead. The other woman obviously misunderstood her nervousness, and put it down to the sudden strain that seemed to be back in Rhea-Jane's relationship with Raff. If only it were that simple!

Rhea-Jane was standing at the day-room window when she saw Jordan's new-style Jaguar turn into the driveway at exactly ten twenty-five, knowing he would have driven the pale blue car himself, hating to give anyone control over his life, even in so small a way.

She felt a certain sisterly pride in him as he stepped out of the car on to the gravel driveway; he was an incredibly handsome individual, completely fit, his dark suit perfectly tailored—as were all his clothes.

He would be an extremely attractive man if he relaxed a little and didn't take life so seriously all the time.

Rhea-Jane's first instinct was to run out into the hallway and open the door to him herself. That would appear strange enough in itself to Mrs Howard, she was sure, but if she launched herself into Jordan's arms, as she longed to do, the other woman was likely to be scandalised, especially as Jordan had supposedly come here to see Raff.

If *Raff* himself were to witness such an affectionate display, the tenuous hold he had over his self-control was likely to break completely!

She could hear the voices out in the hallway, knew Jordan would be asked to wait there while Mrs Howard went to Raff's study to tell him his visitor had arrived, if he weren't already aware of the fact.

The housekeeper had been full of the fact, while she'd poured Rhea-Jane's coffee that morning, that for once Raff hadn't gone straight out to work on the estate after his breakfast.

Rhea-Jane couldn't resist the temptation, while the other woman was absent, of just making Jordan aware of her presence in the house.

Her brother's mouth quirked mockingly as she strolled so confidently out of the day-room. 'Quite an impressive place,' he drawled appreciatively.

She gave an inclination of her head. 'And it could be made even more so.'

'That's what I'm here for,' Jordan nodded.

It wasn't quite what she had meant, but she knew Raff's idea of a leisure complex was the last chance he had to hang on to his estate at all.

'Jordan, I haven't had a chance to tell Raff I'm your sister yet, and I would appreciate it if you didn't do it either.' She looked at him pleadingly, genuinely intending to tell Raff herself who she was, but at a time she thought was right. If ever such a time existed . . .

Jordan looked sceptical too. 'I don't think——'

'Mr Quinlan will see you now, Mr Somerville-Smythe,' Mrs Howard spoke softly behind them, and Rhea-Jane was slightly shamefaced as she turned to face the other woman, wondering just how much of their conversation she had overheard.

Poor Mrs Howard must be confused by a whole series of events that had taken place at the house lately—first Rhea-Jane's unexpected arrival, then the Barnes family deciding to descend on them out of curiosity, and now Jordan. The poor woman must wonder what on earth was going on!

But it was just like Raff to let his housekeeper show Jordan to his study rather than coming out to greet the other man himself, it would put him at an advantage she was sure Jordan was fully aware of; he used these same tactics himself whenever he could!

'I'll talk to you later,' Jordan told her mockingly before following Mrs Howard down the hallway.

Rhea-Jane was even more restless while the two men talked in Raff's study than she had been while waiting for Jordan to arrive. The two men were too much alike, she acknowledged, to actually like each other, but she had a feeling they would respect each other. As long as Raff's prejudice, because of what he believed Rhea-Jane's relationship to be with the other man, didn't jeopardise the interview. If Raff would just give Jordan a chance...

This was ridiculous; neither man would thank her for worrying over him like a mother hen!

But she couldn't help her concern, and the longer the meeting went on the more worried she got, finally going down to the kitchen in the hope that she could be of some help there to take her mind off the two men talking in Raff's study.

When she saw that Mrs Howard was setting up a tray for coffee, Jane knew she had to offer to take the tray up to the two men herself.

'You know Mr Somerville-Smythe, do you?' Mrs Howard made the query casually enough, although she was obviously deeply curious to know exactly what all the unusual happenings were about.

But it wasn't up to Rhea-Jane to enlighten the other woman. 'From London, yes,' she answered economically. 'So I would be pleased to take the tray up for you.' She smiled brightly.

Mrs Howard tilted her head questioningly. 'Shall I put on a third cup?'

Hardly! 'Er—no.' Rhea-Jane did her best to keep a straight face, but it was difficult when she could so easily envisage Raff's fury if she should dare to presume to sit down and drink coffee with himself and Jordan. 'I—they're discussing business,' she added dismissively.

The other woman's curiosity was really aroused now, but Rhea-Jane knew there was no way the other woman would actually ask her what 'business' the two men could be 'discussing'.

She would have liked to be fair, and tell the other woman, but she knew it was up to Raff to tell Mrs Howard if there were to be any changes made on the estate.

There was no guarantee, knowing Raff as she did, that he would agree to Jordan's financial proposals.

It was difficult knocking on a door when holding a tray in one's hands. Jane had never quite appreciated the problem before now, finally resorting to a gentle kick against the polished wood, and hoping Mrs Howard would forgive her for the faint mark her soft leather shoe had left on the wood.

Raff's eyes narrowed as soon as he opened the door and saw it was her standing outside with the laden tray.

'Coffee,' she announced brightly, raising the tray pointedly.

He had no choice but to stand back and let her enter to put the tray down on his desk-top.

Well, that wasn't strictly accurate; he *did* have a choice, but even *he* wouldn't be that rude to her with a third person present in the room!

'Shall I pour?' she offered lightly, smiling at no one in particular, knowing that if she looked directly into Raff's face that he would look furious, and that Jordan would more than probably look amused by her tactics.

'Why not?' Raff closed the door behind her with a firm click. 'I'm sure you know how we both take our coffee.'

Her hand shook slightly as she lifted the coffee-pot; she could tell Raff was more angry than she had ever seen him before, more furious even than he had been the previous evening after talking to Jordan on the telephone.

'And, of course,' Raff continued hardly, 'there's no need to introduce the two of you either, is there?'

'It would be a little ridiculous, in the circumstances.' Jordan was the one to drily answer him as Rhea-Jane seemed to be momentarily struck dumb.

Rhea-Jane swallowed hard, not liking the look of the pulse that beat so angrily in Raff's tightly clenched jaw. Maybe she shouldn't have brought the coffee after all . . . !

'I'll leave the two of you to continue talking,' she told them hastily, turning to leave.

'That won't be necessary,' Raff grated, his eyes glacial when she at last chanced a look at his face, and she turned quickly away again from the antagonism she saw there. 'We've finished talking business, there only remains the question of . . . you.'

She raised startled eyes to his. 'Me?' she echoed dazedly, looking questioningly at Jordan, wondering what he had said to the other man about her, receiving only a puzzled shrug in reply; he no more knew what the other man had meant than she did.

And then Rhea-Jane knew. Of course, Raff still believed she and Jordan were lovers...!

'Yes?' she prompted tensely, her head held back proudly, the hair that so troubled him like a flame down her spine.

'Rhea-Jane will be leaving with me, of course,' Jordan announced arrogantly.

Raff's eyes glittered dangerously as the other man at last revealed her full first name to him. 'Surely that is for—Rhea-Jane to decide?' he challenged softly.

She looked at the two men, realising that they might have come to terms over business—at least, she hoped they had!—but that she, obviously as far as Raff was concerned, was another matter entirely.

She suddenly realised what a bone, that was being fought after by two dogs, must feel like!

Jordan shook his head. 'There can be no question of her staying on here now.'

Raff's mouth tightened at the other man's arrogance, his eyes icy as he looked across at Rhea-Jane. 'Do you want to move back in with him?' he rasped.

What was the alternative? What was Raff offering in its place?

Jordan stood up restlessly, his eyes narrowed. 'Just what has been going on here the last couple of weeks, Rhea? I thought you said this was just a job?'

Her cheeks felt warm, but she was filled with confusion over Raff's behaviour. 'I don't——'

'Do you want to live with him?' Raff cut in harshly, his whole body taut with tension. 'Or stay here with me?'

With him? Was he serious? He looked very serious indeed!

'I don't need saving from myself, Raff, no matter what you may have assumed to the contrary,' she assured him, unable to think of any other reason for his offering to let her stay on here. 'You see, Jordan is——'

'Very wealthy, very influential,' Raff acknowledged grimly. 'But is that really what you want, a rich lover?'

'You know it isn't——'

'I don't have the wealth—yet,' Raff told her grimly. 'Although if the leisure complex venture turns out as profitable as Somerville-Smythe believes it will, that will change in the future. I don't know if you love me, but I do know, from your responses to me, that you aren't in love with *him*.' He nodded in Jordan's direction. 'And I'm willing to offer you marriage, Rhea,' he added challengingly.

Marriage? He wanted to *marry* her?

She looked at him searchingly; he didn't look like a man who had just proposed marriage to her.

Because what he was doing was dangling a gold ring in front of her nose, because he believed it was the one thing Jordan had never offered her!

'Rhea,' Jordan spoke harshly. 'You haven't answered my question.'

And he wanted to know *exactly* what had been 'going on' while she had been staying here, she could tell by his tone of voice that he wouldn't be satisfied with anything less.

'Stop trying to intimidate her,' Raff warned softly. 'She can make her own mind up.'

Jordan looked at him coldly. 'My dear man——'

'I'm not your "dear" anything,' Raff rasped.

'All right—Quinlan,' Jordan bit out in a barely controlled voice. 'I don't know what Rhea has told you about the two of us——' he frowned darkly at Rhea before continuing '—but you seem to be under some misapprehension about our relationship. I am not, nor have I ever been, some sort of rich protector for her. I am, in fact——'

'Jordan, no!' she groaned, knowing everything would change once Raff knew who she really was. And she hadn't answered his suggestion of marriage yet!

Her brother gave her an angry scowl. 'If there was some sort of problem here you should have

corrected it before I arrived this morning,' he criti-
cised harshly. 'I told you last night——'

'Last night?' Raff echoed suspiciously. 'You
telephoned Somerville-Smythe after we talked last
night?'

She grimaced. 'Yes. But I——'

'Just what sort of hold do you have on her?' Raff
turned angrily on the other man.

'No hold, Quinlan,' Jordan told him calmly.
'Just one of the closest relationships possible between a man and a woman. Are you going
to end this ridiculous farce, or am I?' he prompted
Rhea-Jane impatiently.

'The two of you are—married?' Raff said
disbelievingly.

'Hell, no,' Jordan denied derisively. 'If we were
I would have put her over my knee and given her
a good hiding by now! I may still do so,' he added,
looking at her challengingly.

She gave him a dismissive movement of her hand,
moving to stand in front of Raff, putting her hand
on his arm as she looked up at him. 'Do you really
want to marry me?'

'I would hardly have asked you if I hadn't meant
it,' he grated.

Now probably wasn't the time to point out to
him that he hadn't actually *asked* her, just offered
her an alternative to living with Jordan!

'I hope you know what you're doing, Quinlan,'
Jordan muttered. 'I wouldn't wish this hellion on

any man, let alone one I intend having as a business partner. This would be a one-way transition,' he added warningly. 'No trying to give her back once you realise how difficult she is to live with.'

'I'm not difficult to live with——'

'Damned impossible most of the time,' Jordan acknowledged impatiently. 'But maybe she'll make you a better wife than she has me a——'

'Careful, Somerville-Smythe,' Raff warned harshly.

'——sister,' Jordan finished drily.

'Oh, Jordan!' She turned to him, knowing by the way Raff had instantly tensed that he was deeply disturbed by the revelation, that he was more bothered by this than his first assumption about their relationship. 'Raff, I was going to tell you.' She looked up at him imploringly.

He wasn't even looking at her, but staring steadily at Jordan. 'Did you say "sister"?'

'There's little likeness between the two of us, I'll admit,' Jordan nodded. 'Rhea looks like our mother, and I—well, I suppose I must take after my father's side of the family,' he shrugged, because apart from his height he really looked little like their father either; Jordan's colouring was much darker. 'But yes, Rhea is definitely my sister.'

At last Raff looked down at her, and there was such cold disdain in his eyes that Rhea-Jane felt almost as if he had struck her. 'Rhea-Jane

Somerville-Smythe.' The name sounded obscene on his lips.

She swallowed hard. 'If you would just let me explain...'

He pushed her sharply away from him as she would have reached out to him. 'There's nothing to explain,' he told her glacially. 'Whatever little game you've been playing here is over.'

'Raff——'

'I want you to leave here. Now!' he grated harshly, his fury barely leashed, the move to sit down behind his desk seeming to be made more out of a need to put distance between himself and Rhea-Jane than actually to sit down. 'Both of you,' he added flatly.

'But——'

'Rhea, I think it's best if we do go,' Jordan put in quietly, obviously able to gauge the other man's mood as being dangerously close to breaking-point. 'Get your things together, and we'll leave.'

A sob caught in her throat. 'But, Jordan——'

'Now isn't the time, Rhea,' he comforted her, glancing at the stony-faced man who sat so still across the room. 'Definitely not the time,' he repeated with a pointed grimace.

It had all gone so terribly wrong. If she could have just explained to Raff... But Jordan was right, he didn't want to listen now. Maybe when he had calmed down she could just start to explain why she had behaved the way she had. Although looking at his face now, she had a feeling it could be a long time before she could do that.

She felt numbed, and collected her case from her room as if in a dream. Jordan was waiting in the hallway for her, with no sign of the other man, and so she could only assume he was still in his study. Rhea dared not even risk trying to make her goodbyes to Mrs Howard, sure she would break down if she didn't go now; she would have to telephone the other woman once she felt a little stronger.

Saying goodbye to Raff was something she couldn't even think about.

Jordan didn't say a word, just put her case in the back of the car before getting in beside her.

He reached out and squeezed her hands as she clenched them together on her lap. 'You can't blame the man, Rhea,' he soothed. 'At the moment Raff is feeling very humiliated by your deception. Just give him time.'

She just nodded wordlessly, too choked up to speak just yet.

But Jordan's own air of calm was to desert him a few days later!

CHAPTER NINE

'HE's taking this too far!' Jordan stormed into the house, throwing his briefcase down with little regard for the expensive leather, and going straight over to the drinks cabinet to pour himself a glass of whisky, something he rarely did.

Rhea-Jane watched him warily, looking up from the details of property she had been going over for the last few days in an effort to find somewhere suitable for opening up her agency. It didn't look as if it was going to be as simple as she had first thought.

Not that that would stop her; she was determined to do something with her life.

Besides, she had to keep herself busy. So that she didn't dwell on thoughts of Raff.

She was too afraid to let herself even *start* to think about the way they had parted, knew she would break down completely if she did.

She sat back in her chair now, looking across at Jordan. 'What's wrong?' she prompted as he threw the whisky down his throat, his expression grim.

'Quinlan,' he grated.

Rhea-Jane tensed at the mention of his name. 'Raff?' she questioned lightly. 'What has he done to upset you?'

'I instructed my lawyers to send Quinlan all the legal paperwork needed for the business partnership,' Jordan bit out furiously. 'They arrived back today,' he added harshly.

'Yes?' She had tensed expectantly.

'Unsigned!' her brother burst out disgustedly. 'With a terse letter attached to them saying he had changed his mind and decided not to accept my offer after all.' Jordan shook his head. 'The man is a fool. He knows damn well my terms were more than fair.'

But at the time Raff had agreed to the business deal he hadn't known Rhea-Jane's name was Somerville-Smythe too, that she was Jordan's sister. That had to be the reason why he had changed his mind.

And he would lose the estate completely if he didn't do something about his situation soon.

Did he really think it was worth paying that price not to have anything further to do with *her* family?

He had to. God, how he must hate her for her subterfuge!

But she couldn't let him make such a sacrifice out of disgust for her behaviour, she had to try and talk to him.

'*Now* is the time.' She stood up decisively, looking at Jordan challengingly as he realised she meant to go to see Raff. 'He needs this business deal,' she attempted to justify her actions. 'He may regret he ever knew me, but that's no reason to sacrifice everything he's worked for for so many years. I'm going to see Raff now, Jordan,' she stated firmly. 'And don't try and stop me because——'

'I wasn't about to,' he drawled, sitting down in one of the armchairs. 'I put through several telephone calls to Quinlan House today, and each time the housekeeper told me Raff was away.'

'And you don't believe that,' Rhea-Jane sighed.

Jordan raised dark brows. 'Do you?'

No, she didn't; she was sure Raff wouldn't go anywhere at a crucial time like this.

But there was one way to find out, one person she could talk to who might know if Raff was away or not.

She left Jordan in the lounge, and put a call straight through to Robert.

'Well, well,' he began. 'If it isn't Rhea-Jane Somerville-Smythe returned to the fold!'

She groaned. 'You've heard about that?'

'About what?' The frown could be heard in his voice.

'You haven't spoken to Raff?' Rhea-Jane said cautiously, sure, now that she thought about it, that Raff wouldn't have told his family about her.

'Not recently,' Robert drawled. 'One of the crowd said they had seen you in town the other day,' he said carelessly.

'So you wouldn't know if Raff was away at the moment?' she sighed.

'Of course he isn't away,' Robert instantly scorned. 'Raff never leaves his beloved estate.'

She frowned. 'Are you sure?'

'Raff isn't away, believe me.' He sounded hurt by her lack of faith in him. 'Mother would be down there caretaking the place if he was,' he assured her. 'But "the silence has been deafening", to quote a phrase,' he added drily. 'Has Jordan finally agreed to let you have your inheritance, is that why you're back in town?' he continued interestedly.

'Something like that,' she avoided. 'It's just that Raff doesn't seem to be taking calls,' she added worriedly.

'Oh, he often does that,' Robert dismissed unconcernedly. 'Especially if Mother is in one of her bossy moods. But you can depend on it, he's there all right.'

That was what she had thought, she had just wanted it confirmed before driving all the way to Quinlan House.

'What have you done to upset my dear cousin?' Robert probed mockingly. 'Don't tell me, he found out who you are and threw you out!'

She couldn't exactly blame him for his curiosity, but she had no intention of satisfying it!

'You'll have to talk to Raff about that,' she answered evasively again.

'He's as tight-lipped as the proverbial clam, always has been,' Robert grumbled. 'I would be wasting my time asking him anything!'

'You're wasting your time with me, too,' she told him in a bored voice. 'I've got to go now, Robert, but I——'

'Hey, wait a minute!' His hurried protest interrupted her dismissive goodbye. '"One good turn deserves another", and all that.'

'When did you start talking in clichés, Robert?' she taunted. 'It's very boring!'

'That isn't nice, Rhea-Jane,' he complained in a slightly sulky voice, having been convinced for years that he was such a fascinating individual no woman could resist him.

'I'm in a hurry, Robert.' Rhea-Jane sighed her impatience. 'And anyway, you *owed* me a favour after the way you let me down with Jordan,' she reminded him.

'I've explained why I did that,' he wheedled. 'For goodness' sake, Rhea, I only want you to come to a party with me on Saturday night.'

'Why me?' she prompted warily.

He laughed softly, his bad humour gone as quickly as it had arrived; one thing about Robert, he was never in a bad mood for long. 'Do I sense suspicion in your voice?' he taunted.

'In all probability,' she said drily.

'I've invited you out dozens of times in the past, Rhea——'

'I hadn't worked for your cousin then,' Rhea-Jane derided.

'If I promise not to even mention Raff's name, will you come to a party with me on Saturday?' he cajoled.

He was good company when he wanted to be, and he *had* kept quiet about her identity to the rest of the family, much as it must have been a temptation to him not to be... 'Oh, all right,' she conceded without much enthusiasm for the idea.

'You are a love!' Robert's grin could be heard in his voice. 'I'll pick you up about nine o'clock on Saturday night.'

Rhea-Jane rang off, not wasting any more time even thinking about Robert. She could more than handle him, and she had more important things to think about.

Like hoping Raff would be at Quinlan House, as Robert seemed so sure he was.

'I'm going out for a while,' she told Jordan briefly. 'Do you think you could take a look through those?' She pointed at the estate agents' lists on the table. 'You probably know what to look for better than I do.'

And it would help take his mind off Raff!

'But——'

'I have to go, Jordan.' She waved vaguely in his direction, her thoughts already miles away.

Jordan probably knew exactly where she was going, but he wasn't about to deter her!

The two of them had got on a lot better together the last few days, Rhea-Jane having learned a new respect for Jordan and how hard he worked, Jordan seeming to at last accept that she had grown up. They had never mentioned Raff's unexpected offer of marriage, and what Rhea-Jane's answer to it might have been. But the knowledge was there, anyway. They both knew what she would have liked her answer to be.

She and Jordan had never got on so well together, but it was a pity that understanding had come only because she had loved and lost Raff.

She hoped, time and time again, on that drive down to Hampshire, that Robert was right about Raff's being at the estate but just not receiving calls; especially ones from Jordan, Rhea-Jane's brother!

But Raff's actions to her appeared to be a case of 'cutting off his nose to spite his face', and—God, she was getting as bad as Robert with his clichés!

But Raff *was* just being stubborn as far as she could see, was achieving nothing by it, except the possibility of losing the estate to the creditors. And he couldn't really want that, no matter how stubborn he might be feeling at the moment.

Mrs Howard looked surprised to see her when she opened the door to Rhea-Jane's knock, which wasn't surprising, considering the abrupt way she had departed only a few days earlier.

Rhea-Jane hesitated in the doorway. 'Is Raff at home?'

The housekeeper's expression suddenly became evasive. 'Er—well—he is,' she finally admitted awkwardly. 'But——'

'He isn't receiving callers,' Rhea-Jane finished drily, sympathising with the other woman's embarrassment, but so thankful to know that Raff was in the house. 'Don't worry, Mrs Howard——' she touched the other woman's arm reassuringly '—I'll tell him I let myself in,' she promised her as she entered the house.

'But—but——'

'And I'll let myself out again,' she offered, smiling brightly before walking quickly down the hallway towards Raff's study, sure he would be in there, and not wanting to give Mrs Howard time enough to collect her scattered wits, and try to stop her, and forewarn Raff. Forewarned was the last thing she wanted him to be!

She knocked briefly on the study door before entering, having several seconds to look at him before he became aware that it was she who had entered the room, and not Mrs Howard as he had assumed.

The intense feelings of love were quickly followed by anger. He was still working too hard, his face more strained than ever. There was no reason, except his own stubbornness, for him to be pushing himself like this.

'Why have you changed your mind about going ahead with the leisure complex?'

His head had snapped up at the first sound of her voice, his gaze becoming more and more glacial as he looked at her.

He didn't answer her immediately, just sat back in his chair and looked at her.

Rhea-Jane's first impetus had passed, and the longer he looked at her the more uncomfortable she became. And she knew that was exactly what he was hoping to achieve.

But she hadn't taken the trouble to change before coming out, had left immediately the decision was made, before self-doubt could make her change her mind, still wearing the jeans and casual top she had put on that morning to spend the day working at home.

The longer Raff continued to look at her the more she wished she had taken the time to change into one of her 'designer-label' outfits; at least she would have felt more confident in them. Although she didn't think Raff would have found her appearance any more pleasing in the clothing he had been so contemptuous of when they'd first met.

'What,' he finally spoke softly, dangerously so, 'makes you think I've "changed my mind about the leisure complex"?'

Rhea-Jane blinked, frowning. 'But—Jordan said——'

'That I've decided not to follow through on his offer, after all?' Raff finished slowly. 'But that doesn't mean I'm not willing to go into business with someone else.'

Her cheeks had become flushed at the contemptuous way he had said 'his' offer, but her frown deepened at his last remark. 'You're still going ahead with the complex?'

'Of course.' He gave a slight inclination of his head.

He just wasn't interested in going into business with *her* brother, was his unspoken comment!

She moistened her lips. *Now* what was she supposed to say? 'But Jordan's deal,' she finally attempted. 'Surely it was——?'

'I would prefer not to discuss any of that with you,' Raff cut in with cold dismissal.

It was meant as a slap in the face—and it felt like one!

'Now, if you have nothing else to say...?' Raff looked down pointedly at the work on his desk.

'Raff, why won't you at least listen to me?' She went forward pleadingly. 'I know you think I was playing some silly sort of game while I was here, but—but—— Well...'

'Yes?' he prompted hardly.

She swallowed hard. 'I needed a job——'

'With all the Somerville-Smythe millions?' he snorted disbelievingly.

'That's just it,' Rhea-Jane nodded frantically. 'I had——'

He stood up abruptly. 'I'm really not interested, Miss Somerville-Smythe,' he told her coldly. 'And please don't come here trying to interfere in my private business again.' His eyes were narrowed. 'Because it is *my* personal business.'

'You asked me to marry you!' she reminded him out of desperation.

He remained unmoved. 'We all make mistakes.' He began looking through his work, obviously dismissing her.

It was like a physical blow. She knew she had hurt him, but now he was trying to deliberately hurt her. And, although she had half expected it, he was still succeeding.

'It wasn't a mistake, Raff,' she told him with quiet dignity. 'And just for the record——' she paused at the door '——my answer would have been yes.'

She left the room, taking several deep breaths once out in the hallway before walking to the front door, her head back proudly. She might feel like skulking from the house in utter desolation, but she wasn't about to do it.

She managed to leave without bumping into Mrs Howard, which was probably just as well; her emotions were under very tight control, only relaxing slightly once she reached the sanctuary of her car.

And then the tears began to flow, as she acknowledged to herself that she had hoped—and prayed!—Raff would make some attempt to stop her leaving.

She should have known better.

Jordan was still up when she got in and, much as she didn't feel like being seen by anyone just now, she knew she at least owed Jordan an explanation.

He was still in the lounge, although he had obviously eaten his dinner in her absence. He looked up at her expectantly.

Rhea-Jane sighed. 'I failed to talk any sense into Raff—you will have gathered that's where I've been?' She grimaced.

Her brother shrugged. 'I guessed it might have been, yes.'

'He didn't even want to begin to listen to me, I'm afraid,' she revealed dully.

'Rhea——' He broke off as the doorbell rang, and the two of them frowned at each other.

It was ten o'clock at night; who on earth could be calling at this time?

'I'll get it.' Jordan stood up. 'I told Henson we wouldn't need him any more tonight,' he explained before leaving the room.

Rhea-Jane was glad of the respite which gave her the opportunity to gather her shattered emotions. Jordan wasn't stupid, he could easily guess at all the things she hadn't yet told him about her visit to Raff.

She turned as she heard him enter the lounge again. 'Jordan, I——' The words froze in her throat as she saw the man standing at Jordan's side.

Raff...

CHAPTER TEN

RHEA-JANE, who had been home only a few minutes, couldn't believe Raff was here now. He had to have left Quinlan House almost immediately after her to have got here so quickly.

He was looking at her intently, a nerve pulsing in his cheek, his body filled with nervous energy.

Nervous? *Raff?*

She frowned her puzzlement at his behaviour. What was he *doing* here? Not two hours ago he had left her in no doubt as to how he felt about seeing her again.

'I came to accept your offer,' he finally said, his voice strained. 'If it still stands,' he added uncertainly.

She shrugged. 'I'm sure Jordan is still interested in——'

'I'm not talking about the leisure complex,' Raff cut in harshly. 'A short time ago you told me you would have accepted my marriage proposal if I had let you give me an answer. I've come to accept your acceptance.'

Jordan gave a brief laugh, shaking his head at the two of them. 'I think I had better leave you two alone to talk; it all sounds a little complicated to me.' He turned to leave.

167

'Oh, but Jordan,' Rhea-Jane stopped him, frowning. 'Don't you want to talk to Raff?'

He glanced at the other man. 'I believe it can wait. It's already waited this long, a few more hours isn't going to make a lot of difference. Besides,' he added teasingly, 'I think the two of you had better sort out this marriage proposal before either of you changes your mind again!'

There was an awkward pause after Jordan had left the room, neither Raff nor Rhea-Jane seeming to know what to say to each other now they were alone.

But Raff had followed her, after all!

It had taken him a little longer than she would have wished, he had put her through fresh heartbreak, but he was here.

'I want it clearly understood,' Raff suddenly rasped, 'that I won't touch a penny of your money. You can do what you like with it, but I never want it said I married you for your money.'

'Raff——'

'Because I'm *not* marrying you for your money. In fact——'

'Raff, the way things stand, at this moment in time I don't *have* any money,' she cut in firmly, relieved to see she at last had his full attention. '*That's* why I needed a job, why I—— Oh, God, it's a long story,' she frowned, and then proceeded to tell him of her father's will and the conditions attached to it.

'Damn fool,' Raff muttered, hands thrust into his trouser-pockets.

'Not really.' She grimaced. 'I was a headstrong little madam until I reached eighteen, which was when my father died.'

Raff gave a wry smile. '*Was* a headstrong little madam?' he taunted.

Rhea-Jane returned his smile, a bubble of happiness starting to rise inside her. 'If you think I'm bad now you should have known me three years ago!'

'I would have liked to.' He spoke gruffly. 'Rhea, did you mean what you said earlier, about marrying me?' He stood in front of her, his eyes dark with emotion.

'I meant it,' she nodded.

His hands came up to cup each side of her face. 'Will you do me the honour of marrying me?'

'Oh, yes!' She threw her arms up about his neck, feeling as if she had come home.

They kissed with a thirst that seemed as if it might never be assuaged, over and over again, desire licking through their bodies, both of them trembling with need as they moved slightly apart.

'I've missed you so much these last few days,' Raff admitted gruffly.

'I've hated it.' Rhea-Jane shook her head at the unnecessary suffering they had both been through.

'I just felt such a damned fool,' Raff sighed, grimacing. 'There was I telling this rich and powerful man that I wanted to marry you and he couldn't have you, and you turned out to be his *sister*, and just as rich and powerful!'

'But——'

'I know you aren't really like that, darling,' he smiled down at her. 'If you were, you would have told me several times in the last few weeks exactly what I could do with my job. I know you said you needed the job, but you didn't need my insults too,' he realised self-derisively as she would have protested. 'Once I realised who you really were I——'

'No more self-recriminations.' Rhea-Jane's fingertips on his lips stopped him. 'We're together now. And nothing else will drive us apart, will it?' she added a little anxiously.

His arms tightened about her. 'I promise to try not to behave like a stubborn fool again,' he derided himself.

'And I promise—— Oh, dear!' She gave a sudden frown. 'Now I don't want you to be cross, but I— well, I've agreed to go to a party with Robert on Saturday evening.' She smiled grimly.

Raff's brows rose. 'In that case, I take it he knew all along exactly who you were?'

'I'm afraid so, although I swore him to secrecy,' she hastened to explain.

Raff's mouth quirked. 'Then by all means keep your date with him on Saturday night; it will be a case of "your fiancé came too"! It might be a good idea if Jordan accompanies us as well,' he added thoughtfully.

'Isn't that being a little too cruel?' Rhea-Jane
protested laughingly. 'One of you Robert might be
able to cope with, two of you just wouldn't be fair!'

Raff shrugged. 'The party he is taking you to is
undoubtedly Anita and Jack's anniversary bash; it
will be the ideal time to announce our engagement
and introduce you and Jordan to the rest of the
family,' he explained.

'Your aunt isn't going to be pleased,' Rhea-Jane
said soberly, remembering the other woman's
coldness towards her.

'Anita's opinion has never been of importance
to me before, so I don't see why I should change
the habit of a lifetime,' Raff dismissed.

But none of them was quite prepared for Anita
Barnes's reaction when she discovered exactly who
Rhea-Jane was!

Robert arrived exactly on time to pick her up for
their date on Saturday evening, coming to an abrupt
halt when she showed him through to the lounge
and he came face to face with the other two men.

Raff had more or less moved in over the last
couple of days, most of their time having been spent
together, Raff more relaxed now, the strain gone
from his face, Rhea-Jane knowing that her own face
glowed with happiness.

The three men together were enough to take any
woman's breath away, all so tall and handsome,
and very attractive in their dinner-suits and white

shirts. Rhea-Jane felt privileged to be escorted by three such dashing men.

Although Robert still wasn't aware of the fact that she *was* going to be escorted by all three of them! Poor Robert.

'Er—Jordan,' he acknowledged abruptly. 'Raff...' he added in a puzzled voice.

Raff glanced at the plain watch on his wrist. 'I see you can be punctual when a beautiful woman is involved,' he drawled.

'Do you want a drink first or shall we be on our way?' Jordan offered politely, looking at them enquiringly.

Robert's eyes widened. 'We? But——'

'I don't think it's safe to let my fiancée out alone with you,' Raff told him lightly.

'And just to make sure, I'm coming along too,' Jordan explained mockingly.

Raff and Jordan had become a formidable duo the last few days.

From a business angle the partnership was moving along nicely, and, to Rhea-Jane's surprise, on a personal level the two men were becoming the best of friends. Poor Robert didn't stand a chance when they joined forces.

'Fiancée?' Robert looked totally stunned by this piece of information. 'But you didn't say anything the other night when I——'

'Oh, we weren't engaged then,' Raff informed him dismissively, his arm going gently about Rhea-Jane's shoulders as he drew her to his side. 'Rhea had already agreed to go out with you when she consented to be my wife. Of course, she didn't want to let you down at such short notice,' he continued, 'but in the circumstances I don't——'

'Oh, I'll be only too happy to have you accompany us,' Robert assured him hastily, obviously reconciling himself to the situation, perhaps even coming to enjoy it a little; after all, there was his mother to tell the good news to yet! 'You too, Jordan, of course,' he added with largesse.

By the time they reached the Barneses' home Rhea-Jane could see Robert was clearly aware of all the possibilities the next few minutes could bring, and that he was greatly looking forward to the upset the announcement of Raff's engagement to Rhea-Jane was going to cause the rest of the family.

Robert had always known he would never be any more than a friend to Rhea-Jane himself, so she certainly hadn't expected him to be upset on that count, and now he was over the first shock of realising she was going to be his cousin-in-law he was enjoying himself immensely.

The driveway to the Barneses' house was full of Mercedeses, BMWs, Jaguars, and there was even one majestic Rolls-Royce.

'Just a few family friends,' Robert teased as he parked his sporty car out on the road.

'Now you know why I usually avoid these affairs,' Raff muttered to Rhea-Jane as he opened the door for her to step out of the car beside him on the pavement.

'Never mind——' she put her arm through the crook of his, reaching up to kiss him lingeringly on the lips '—the next party you'll have to go to is our wedding.'

'Next month?' he urged gruffly.

They had talked over possible dates for the wedding, and as far as Rhea-Jane and Raff were concerned it could be tomorrow, but Jordan insisted Rhea-Jane should have a proper wedding, with the right amount of notice given to family and friends. He was also adamant that it should be a church wedding, and that he would give her away. Rhea-Jane had teased him about the latter, claiming he would probably force Raff to take her if he could!

'As soon as it can be arranged,' she promised.

'Come on, you two,' Robert urged them impatiently. 'You'll have time for all that later.'

Rhea-Jane laughed softly as they followed him to the house. 'You can hardly wait to make the announcement, can you?' she taunted.

He turned to grin at her. 'No!'

'He's honest, anyway,' Jordan drawled as he brought up the rear.

Raff gave him a meaningful glance. 'You haven't met my aunt Anita yet,' he warned.

'I'm looking forward to it,' Jordan muttered as the door was opened by a young girl of about sixteen who, with her cascade of dark hair, bore a distinct resemblance to Robert.

'So am I,' Raff murmured with amusement.

Anita Barnes was at the centre of what Rhea-Jane could only describe as a 'glittering' crowd of people, the glitter mainly coming from the jewels the middle-aged women were adorned with.

But as soon as Anita saw Robert she excused herself and crossed the room to greet him.

The older woman looked almost pretty tonight, a happy glow to her austere features, an affectionate smile curving her lips as she reached up to kiss her only son. 'Thank you for the beautiful flowers you sent, darling,' she told him warmly. 'Your father is about somewhere...' She gave a dismissive gesture in the direction of the crowded sitting-room behind her.

'I'll see him in a minute,' Robert nodded. 'Right now, Mother, I'd like to——'

'Raff!' Anita had finally seen him standing slightly to one side behind Robert. 'How lovely of you to come,' she added in a rather puzzled voice, as if seeing him here was the last thing she had expected. As it probably was! 'I had no idea you knew——'

'Raff came with me, Mother,' Robert cut in firmly, obviously slightly put out at having his announcement interrupted.

'He did?' Anita looked even more puzzled, knowing the two of them had never really been close.

'And his fiancée,' Robert added softly.

'His——?' Some of the gaiety left Anita Barnes's face, her eyes widening as she saw Rhea-Jane standing at Raff's side. 'But—but you're——'

'Rhea-Jane Somerville-Smythe,' Robert told her with relish.

'No...!' his mother protested weakly, paling.

'And this is her brother——'

'Jordan,' Anita finished faintly, what little colour had been left in her face after Rhea-Jane had been formally introduced fading rapidly as she looked disbelievingly at Jordan. 'How—what—how did you find out? Did she leave you a letter or something like that? And after telling me no one would ever find out!'

She turned accusingly to Rhea-Jane. 'And how dare you sneak into the family home in that way? Jane Smith, indeed!' she snorted. 'And I even commented that weekend on how like Diana you were,' she added self-disgustedly. 'How you must have laughed at me. What did you do it for, that's what I would like to know? There's no money, you know.' She gave a harsh laugh. 'Good God, with the Somerville-Smythe millions why should you be interested in the little there is in the estate? You——'

'Anita!' Jack Barnes cut in forcefully, keeping a tight smile on his lips for the benefit of the audience to this conversation his wife's outburst had aroused, and taking a firm hold of her arm. 'Keep your voice down,' he muttered. 'If there's some problem let's all go into my study and discuss it.'

'But——'

'I think Jack is right, Anita,' Raff put in harshly, his narrowed gaze on his aunt's face.

Rhea-Jane was still stunned by the vehemence of the attack, trembling slightly as Raff's arm moved protectively about her waist. A little outrage on the other woman's part, on account of her deceit, was to be expected, but this was something else!

Jack Barnes's study bore little resemblance to either Raff's or Jordan's, being meticulously tidy, decorated in blues and greys probably of his wife's choosing.

Anita waited only long enough for the door to be closed behind her before turning on, of all people, Jordan this time. 'You have no claim on the family estate, you know,' she scorned. 'Not without running the risk of losing all that Somerville-Smythe left you. And——'

'Anita!' Raff's quietly authoritative voice silenced the tirade. 'Jordan is about to become my brother-in-law.'

'The damned irony of it!' his aunt scoffed disgustedly. 'But then, I suppose for respectability's sake it couldn't have worked out better,' she scorned, turning flashing eyes on Rhea-Jane. 'I should have known you were *her* daughter. The likeness...' She shook her head frustratedly. 'You seem destined to make fools of the men in this family, no matter what the barriers might be!'

Raff moved forward, a nerve pulsing in his cheek. 'Anita, I want you to tell me what the hell you're talking about.'

Her gaze swept scathingly over Rhea-Jane and Jordan. 'Why don't you ask them?'

His gaze didn't waver. 'Because I'm asking you.'

'The little fool was pregnant when she left Quinlan House,' Anita announced distastefully. 'Such an innocent, she got herself pregnant!'

Raff stiffened at Rhea-Jane's side. 'Rhea-Jane is not pregnant,' he said with certainty.

'I'm not talking about *her*,' Anita dismissed scathingly.

'My mother,' Jordan put in huskily. 'She's talking about my mother.'

'You see, he knows what I'm talking about,' Anita pounced triumphantly. 'The little fool didn't want to get rid of it, but by this time Donald's responsibilities lay with Helen, seriously injured after a car accident, and so I offered to help Diana out.'

'How?' Raff demanded harshly.

'Financially,' his aunt snapped. 'Until she could decide what she was going to do about the baby——'

'She kept it,' Jordan put in softly, looking as if he were made of stone, he stood so still.

'She kept *you*, yes.' Anita glared at him. 'What do you want from us now?' she demanded to know. 'You have more now than you would ever have got with Donald as your father!'

It was all so incredible.

It couldn't be true, could it, what Anita Barnes was undoubtedly saying?

Jordan was Raff's *brother* . . .?

Because that was *exactly* what the other woman was saying.

'They've made a fool of you, Raff,' Anita told him scornfully. 'Little Miss Smith here coming to live in Quinlan House pretending she needed a job, when all the time——'

'Mrs Barnes,' Jordan cut in coldly. 'Fantastic as it might seem, Rhea is a complete innocent in all this.'

'You don't really expect me to believe that?' Anita said scathingly.

'I expect you to believe,' Jordan's voice was at its most dangerously soft, 'that until a few minutes ago neither Rhea nor myself, nor indeed Raff—if his stunned expression is anything to go by—had any idea that Donald Quinlan was . . . my father.' For all his hauteur, Jordan was obviously dazed by the knowledge, too.

As well he might be—it was incredible!

Anita looked at the three of them, really looked at the three of them for the first time, seeing the truth of Jordan's words there in their faces. 'Oh, God,' she breathed weakly. 'You mean, if I hadn't said anything——'

'As you appear not to have done all these years,' Raff put in harshly.

'—none of you would ever have known,' Anita realised heavily, all the fight seeming to have gone out of her at this realisation. 'Oh, God,' she groaned, grasping the back of the chair that stood in front of the desk. 'When I saw the three of you together I thought you must have somehow found out the truth and come here to confront me with it.'

'I think,' Raff stated firmly, 'that now you have gone this far you had better tell us exactly what that truth is!'

Anita closed her eyes briefly. 'The two of you are really going to be married?' She looked at Rhea-Jane and Raff.

'As soon as it can be arranged,' Raff nodded tersely.

Anita sighed, moving to sit down. 'Then you'll have to know the truth, won't you?' she accepted dully. 'You know, for years Diana and I would avoid being at the same social occasions.' She shook her head. 'And now this!'

Rhea-Jane moved to Raff's side as Anita began to tell them what had happened thirty years ago.

Donald and Helen Quinlan were separated when Diana went to the house as Raff's nanny, Helen having left some months previously with the family chauffeur, claiming she had had enough of the boring life to be had there.

Rhea-Jane felt Raff tense at this, and her hand caressed his arm to show him she understood the dismay this conversation was giving him.

The inevitable had happened. Donald and Diana fell in love.

It was obvious, from Anita's scornful attitude, how she had felt about that!

'You would have approved of that, I dare say?' Anita accused Raff.

'And obviously you wouldn't?' he rasped.

Anita's turned back with derision. 'Diana was even more unsuitable as mistress of Quinlan House than Helen had been!'

'In whose opinion?' Raff challenged.

'You know how I've always felt about Quinlan House,' his aunt defended.

He nodded. 'To the point where no one was good enough to own the estate but you!'

Anita's face was flushed. 'I have as much right——'

'I don't think there's any point in getting involved in personalities, Anita,' Jack Barnes cut in quietly, obviously as stunned by his wife's revelations as the rest of them. 'Just stick to the facts,' he encouraged uncomfortably.

'Very well,' she accepted snappily. 'Helen was injured in a car accident, paralysed from the waist down. Her young lover deserted her without a qualm, apparently,' she added distastefully. 'What could poor Donald do in the circumstances?' she shrugged. 'He suddenly had a wife, the mother of his son, who needed him very badly.'

'And Diana was expecting his child,' Raff bit out, glancing at Jordan, who stood so white-faced and still across the room.

'Donald never knew about that——'

'*What?*' Raff demanded incredulously.

'Diana hadn't had a chance to tell him, when Helen's accident happened,' Anita explained impatiently. 'Donald would never have ignored the existence of his son if he had known about him,' she defended.

'*You* knew,' Raff accused.

'Only because I had seen Diana being ill one day and guessed at the truth,' his aunt told him defensively. 'But she swore me to secrecy...'

'A secret you were only too happy to keep,' Raff taunted harshly.

'Raff!' Jack Barnes cautioned. 'This isn't helping the situation.' He glanced pointedly at Jordan.

'No,' Raff accepted impatiently.

Anita drew in a deep breath. 'Diana decided she had to leave, and because of Helen's presence back in the house Donald had no choice but to accept her decision. I felt almost sorry for Diana, offered to help her out if I could. Then by some fluke she met Somerville-Smythe,' she said disgustedly. 'He couldn't have children of his own, Diana was pregnant but alone; it was a perfect match,' Anita dismissed scathingly.

'But—but that can't be possible,' Rhea-Jane protested that claim. 'There's me!'

Anita looked at her assessingly. 'So there is,' she drawled speculatively. 'And undoubtedly Diana's daughter.'

'And James's daughter, too,' Jordan assured Rhea-Jane calmly, the first time he had spoken since

Anita had begun her explanation. 'I can still remember his behaviour when you were born.' He shook his head. 'There was grief that he had lost Mother, but at the same time he went around the house ranting and raving about it "only being a damned girl after all these years of trying". It didn't make sense to me at the time, but it does now.'

And Rhea-Jane realised now that her father had never forgiven her for 'only being a damned girl'. She had been his first legitimate child, and not the boy he had hoped for! It explained so much of his behaviour towards her.

In fact, all of this explained so much...

'And my father and mother lived the rest of their married life in armed neutrality,' Raff sighed. 'What a damned waste!'

'But your Rhea-Jane wouldn't have been born if Donald and Diana had stayed together all those years ago,' Anita pointed out mockingly.

His arm tightened about Rhea-Jane's shoulders. 'Then for our sakes I can only be glad it worked out the way that it did. But——'

'Mummy!' The young brunette who had originally opened the door to them entered the room after the briefest of knocks. 'Your guests are getting a little restless at your disappearance. After all, it 's your anniversary party!'

'We're coming now, Chelsea,' her father assured her firmly. 'Anita, Robert, I see it's time we rejoined the party.' He turned to Raff, Jordan, and

Rhea-Jane. 'I think the three of you need to be alone to talk.'

'But, Jack——'

'Anita, I think your silence all these years has caused enough damage,' he reproved his wife in an uncharacteristic show of strength where she was concerned. 'The least we can do now is leave these three young people alone to become accustomed to their change of relationship.'

Anita followed her husband disgruntledly, Robert giving Rhea-Jane an encouraging smile before exiting himself.

Raff and Jordan simply stared at each other once they had been left alone in the silence of the study, and Rhea-Jane recalled all the times she had compared the two men and found them to be so much alike. There was a similarity in their looks too, she realised now, although she had obviously never looked for such a likeness before.

Raff was the first to speak. 'Despite her designs on the Quinlan estate I can't believe Anita kept all that to herself for thirty years.' He shook his head a little dazedly. 'If Rhea-Jane and I hadn't met . . .'

'But we did,' she reminded him firmly.

'Fate.' Jordan finally spoke. 'It had to happen,' he added convincingly. 'And I have a feeling that Mother would have been very happy about it.'

'Jordan——'

'Would the two of you excuse me?' Jordan interrupted Rhea-Jane in a strained voice as she would have gone to his side. 'I—I need time to be alone and—think about all this.'

'But——'

'Let him go, Rhea.' Raff softly stopped her, watching the other man as he crossed to the door with jerky movements. 'He needs time on his own,' he advised gently after Jordan had left. 'Time to think, as he said. Time to reassess his own position.'

'Oh, Raff.' Rhea-Jane buried her face against his chest. 'I can't believe all this.'

'Then how do you think Jordan feels?' he cajoled. 'Hey, come on, Rhea, it will all work out, you'll see,' he soothed as she trembled.

'How could Anita have kept such a thing to herself all these years?' She shook her head disbelievingly.

'At a guess I would say I was just about right when I suggested she didn't want another child on the scene ruining Robert's chances of one day inheriting the estate,' Raff drawled.

Rhea-Jane looked up at him. 'You know about that?'

'Of course,' he dismissed, some of his own shock starting to fade. 'And until I met you there was never any chance of her plans being foiled.' He smiled down at her.

'And they're foiled twice over now that Jordan knows he's your—brother.' She shook her head. 'That's going to take a little getting used to! And we could have children of our own. I'd like that,' she added wistfully.

'So would I.' Raff's arms tightened about her. 'Maybe once we have a child, whom we can all share in, Jordan included, this change of relationship won't seem so strange to us.'

'Let's hope not,' she said worriedly, knowing what a blow the last half-hour had been to Jordan; in a sense he had lost his own identity. He was going to need all the loving support they could give him over the next few months.

'We'll support each other.' Raff accurately read her concern. 'It will work out, Rhea.'

And when he spoke as positively as that she couldn't doubt him!

EPILOGUE

'MY MOTHER still isn't pleased,' Robert told her drily.

Rhea-Jane smiled up at him as they danced together in the main salon of the house, the furniture cleared from the room to allow for the fifty or so guests invited to celebrate her twenty-first birthday with her. 'She looks a little happier than she did at the wedding last month.' She glanced across to where Anita Barnes was at least trying to look as if she were enjoying herself—even if she was convincing very few people of the fact!

It had been a busy month, work due to begin on the estate directly after this party, Raff and Jordan partners in the venture, their relationship known only to close family. After all, the marriage between Rhea and Raff had made the two men brothers-in-law, and it had been accepted as natural that the two men should go into business together.

'"Family silver", and all that,' he reminded her.

Rhea-Jane laughed softly. 'She's going to be even more upset when she knows about the baby.'

'My God, you aren't—you don't mean——?' Robert stopped dancing to stare down at her. 'Already?'

'Already,' she glowed up at him, ecstatic with the news. 'Raff is absolutely delighted,' she added happily.

'You certainly didn't waste any time!' Robert looked admiring.

The first night of their honeymoon, to be exact...

Diana's grandchild would be born into the Quinlan family, surrounded by the love of its mother and father.

'If you aren't going to dance with my wife, then I will,' Raff told the younger man, whisking Rhea-Jane away among the other couples dancing before Robert could even think of raising any objections.

She smiled up at him lovingly. 'I think Robert is going to enjoy telling his mother about the baby,' she said with relish.

Raff grinned. 'I wouldn't be at all surprised. I've just had the pleasure of telling Jordan. He wants to know if he's going to be known as Uncle Uncle Jordan, as the baby will make him an uncle twice over?'

'I never thought of that!' she laughed.

Raff sobered slightly. 'He's going to be just fine, you know.'

She looked across to where Jordan was in polite conversation with one of Raff's elderly maiden aunts. There could be no doubting that finding out that Donald Quinlan was his father and not James Somerville-Smythe, as he had always thought, had knocked him for six, but he slowly seemed to be adjusting to the fact.

'We'll make sure he is,' Rhea-Jane agreed warmly.

'God, you're lovely.' Raff looked down at her darkly. 'Do we have to stay here? Can't we just slip away and be alone together?'

She moved closer to him. 'We've been "slipping away to be alone together" the last nine weeks,' she reminded him ruefully. 'We really should make an effort to behave ourselves tonight.'

Marriage suited both of them; theirs was a loving relationship, a true partnership, because although Raff refused to touch any of her money they were, in fact, working together with Jordan on the leisure complex, would run it together once everything was completed: Rhea-Jane had found her niche in life, after all.

'We've made an effort—and failed,' Raff coaxed. 'Come on, Rhea,' he encouraged. 'It *is* your birthday today, darling. I think reaching the age of twenty-one deserves to be celebrated—privately.'

'Later,' she promised.

'Now,' he insisted softly.

Rhea-Jane looked up at him, loving every hard contour of his face, recognising the desire she could see there, knowing that same desire herself.

'Now,' she agreed huskily, knowing that their fated attraction had turned into something so much more special, that it would last a lifetime.

IT'S FREE! IT'S FUN! ENTER THE

☆ "Hooray for ☆
☆ Hollywood" ☆
SWEEPSTAKES!

We're giving away prizes to celebrate the screening of four new romance movies on CBS TV this fall! Look for the movies on four Sunday afternoons in October. And be sure to return your Official Entry Coupons to try for a fabulous vacation in Hollywood!

 If you're the Grand Prize winner we'll fly you and your companion to Los Angeles for a 7-day/6-night vacation you'll never forget!

 You'll stay at the luxurious Regent Beverly Wilshire Hotel,* a prime location for celebrity spotting!

 You'll have time to visit Universal Studios,* stroll the Hollywood Walk of Fame, check out celebrities' footprints at Mann's Chinese Theater, ride a trolley to see the homes of the stars, and more!

 The prize includes a rental car for 7 days and $1,000.00 pocket money!

Someone's going to win this fabulous prize, and it might just be you! Remember, the more times you enter, the better your chances of winning!

 Five hundred entrants will each receive SUNGLASSES OF THE STARS! Don't miss out. ENTER TODAY!

Take 4 bestselling love stories FREE

Plus get a FREE surprise gift!

Special Limited-time Offer

Mail to Harlequin Reader Service®

3010 Walden Avenue
P.O. Box 1867
Buffalo, N.Y. 14269-1867

YES! Please send me 4 free Harlequin Presents® novels and my free surprise gift. Then send me 6 brand-new novels every month, which I will receive months before they appear in bookstores. Bill me at the low price of $2.44 each plus 25¢ delivery and applicable sales tax, if any*. That's the complete price and—compared to the cover prices of $2.99 each—quite a bargain! I understand that accepting the books and gift places me under no obligation ever to buy any books. I can always return a shipment and cancel at any time. Even if I never buy another book from Harlequin, the 4 free books and the surprise gift are mine to keep forever.

106 BPA ANRH

Name	(PLEASE PRINT)	
Address	Apt. No.	
City	State	Zip

This offer is limited to one order per household and not valid to present Harlequin Presents® subscribers. *Terms and prices are subject to change without notice. Sales tax applicable in N.Y.

UPRES-84R   ©1990 Harlequin Enterprises Limited

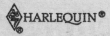

The movie event of the season can be the reading event of the year!

Lights... The lights go on in October when CBS presents Harlequin/Silhouette Sunday Matinee Movies. These four movies are based on bestselling Harlequin and Silhouette novels.

Camera... As the cameras roll, be the first to read the original novels the movies are based on!

Action..: Through this offer, you can have these books sent directly to you! Just fill in the order form below and you could be reading the books...before the movie!

48288-4	Treacherous Beauties by Cheryl Emerson		
	$3.99 U.S./$4.50 CAN.	☐
83305-9	Fantasy Man by Sharon Green		
	$3.99 U.S./$4.50 CAN.	☐
48289-2	A Change of Place by Tracy Sinclair		
	$3.99 U.S./$4.50CAN.	☐
83306-7	Another Woman by Margot Dalton		
	$3.99 U.S./$4.50 CAN.	☐

TOTAL AMOUNT	$
POSTAGE & HANDLING	$
($1.00 for one book, 50¢ for each additional)	
APPLICABLE TAXES*	$_____
TOTAL PAYABLE	$_____
(check or money order—please do not send cash)	

To order, complete this form and send it, along with a check or money order for the total above, payable to Harlequin Books, to: **In the U.S.:** 3010 Walden Avenue, P.O. Box 9047, Buffalo, NY 14269-9047; **In Canada:** P.O. Box 613, Fort Erie, Ontario, L2A 5X3.

Name: _____

Address: _____ City: _____

State/Prov.: _____ Zip/Postal Code: _____

*New York residents remit applicable sales taxes.
Canadian residents remit applicable GST and provincial taxes.

CBSPR

"HOORAY FOR HOLLYWOOD" SWEEPSTAKES

HERE'S HOW THE SWEEPSTAKES WORKS

OFFICIAL RULES — NO PURCHASE NECESSARY

To enter, complete an Official Entry Form or hand print on a 3" x 5" card the words "HOORAY FOR HOLLYWOOD", your name and address and mail your entry in the pre-addressed envelope (if provided) or to: "Hooray for Hollywood" Sweepstakes, P.O. Box 9076, Buffalo, NY 14269-9076 or "Hooray for Hollywood" Sweepstakes, P.O. Box 637, Fort Erie, Ontario L2A 5X3. Entries must be sent via First Class Mail and be received no later than 12/31/94. No liability is assumed for lost, late or misdirected mail.

Winners will be selected in random drawings to be conducted no later than January 31, 1995 from all eligible entries received.

Grand Prize: A 7-day/6-night trip for 2 to Los Angeles, CA including round trip air transportation from commercial airport nearest winner's residence, accommodations at the Regent Beverly Wilshire Hotel, free rental car, and $1,000 spending money. (Approximate prize value which will vary dependent upon winner's residence: $5,400.00 U.S.); 500 Second Prizes: A pair of "Hollywood Star" sunglasses (prize value: $9.95 U.S. each). Winner selection is under the supervision of D.L. Blair, Inc., an independent judging organization, whose decisions are final. Grand Prize travelers must sign and return a release of liability prior to traveling. Trip must be taken by 2/1/96 and is subject to airline schedules and accommodations availability.

Sweepstakes offer is open to residents of the U.S. (except Puerto Rico) and Canada who are 18 years of age or older, except employees and immediate family members of Harlequin Enterprises, Ltd., its affiliates, subsidiaries, and all agencies, entities or persons connected with the use, marketing or conduct of this sweepstakes. All federal, state, provincial, municipal and local laws apply. Offer void wherever prohibited by law. Taxes and/or duties are the sole responsibility of the winners. Any litigation within the province of Quebec respecting the conduct and awarding of prizes may be submitted to the Regie des loteries et courses du Quebec. All prizes will be awarded; winners will be notified by mail. No substitution of prizes are permitted. Odds of winning are dependent upon the number of eligible entries received.

Potential grand prize winner must sign and return an Affidavit of Eligibility within 30 days of notification. In the event of non-compliance within this time period, prize may be awarded to an alternate winner. Prize notification returned as undeliverable may result in the awarding of prize to an alternate winner. By acceptance of their prize, winners consent to use of their names, photographs, or likenesses for purpose of advertising, trade and promotion on behalf of Harlequin Enterprises, Ltd., without further compensation unless prohibited by law. A Canadian winner must correctly answer an arithmetical skill-testing question in order to be awarded the prize.

For a list of winners (available after 2/28/95), send a separate stamped, self-addressed envelope to: Hooray for Hollywood Sweepstakes 3252 Winners, P.O. Box 4200, Blair, NE 68009.

CBSRLS

OFFICIAL ENTRY COUPON

"Hooray for Hollywood"
SWEEPSTAKES!

Yes, I'd love to win the Grand Prize — a vacation in Hollywood — or one of 500 pairs of "sunglasses of the stars"! Please enter me in the sweepstakes!

This entry must be received by December 31, 1994.
Winners will be notified by January 31, 1995.

Name _____

Address _____ Apt. _____

City _____

State/Prov. _____ Zip/Postal Code _____

Daytime phone number _____
(area code)

Mail all entries to: Hooray for Hollywood Sweepstakes,
P.O. Box 9076, Buffalo, NY 14269-9076.
In Canada, mail to: Hooray for Hollywood Sweepstakes,
P.O. Box 637, Fort Erie, ON L2A 5X3.

KCH

OFFICIAL ENTRY COUPON

"Hooray for Hollywood"
SWEEPSTAKES!

Yes, I'd love to win the Grand Prize — a vacation in Hollywood — or one of 500 pairs of "sunglasses of the stars"! Please enter me in the sweepstakes!

This entry must be received by December 31, 1994.
Winners will be notified by January 31, 1995.

Name _____

Address _____ Apt. _____

City _____

State/Prov. _____ Zip/Postal Code _____

Daytime phone number _____
(area code)

Mail all entries to: Hooray for Hollywood Sweepstakes,
P.O. Box 9076, Buffalo, NY 14269-9076.
In Canada, mail to: Hooray for Hollywood Sweepstakes,
P.O. Box 637, Fort Erie, ON L2A 5X3.

KCH